Heat fogged her mind and she gave in to the new sensations, revelling in this strange awakening of a physical self she barely knew.

In the end, the kiss stopped as suddenly as it had started, Nick breaking the contact, leaning back against the wall beside her and mopping his brow with the back of his hand—an extravagant gesture supported by his hearty, 'Phew!'

'Talk about still waters,' he muttered, squinting suspiciously at her from his position against the wall. 'If you've been kissing poor old Charles like that, no wonder the guy's confused.'

Before she had time to tell him she'd never kissed Charles, or anyone else for that matter, with the wanton abandon she'd so recently displayed, he pushed himself upright and walked away. When he reached the door leading into his office, he opened it, then turned back towards her.

'OK,' he said, his voice so calm she realised he'd almost certainly exaggerated the kiss-reaction, 'what shall we do for an encore?'

As a person who lists her hobbies as 'reading, reading and reading', it was hardly surprising **Meredith Webber** fell into writing when she needed a job she could do at home. Not that anyone in the family considers it a 'real' job! She is fortunate enough to live on the Gold Coast in Queensland, Australia, as this gives her the opportunity to catch up with many other people with the same 'unreal' job when they visit the popular tourist area.

Recent titles by the same author:

REDEEMING DR HAMMOND
CLAIMED: ONE WIFE
FOUND: ONE HUSBAND
HEART'S COMMAND

A VERY PRECIOUS GIFT

BY
MEREDITH WEBBER

*First published in Great Britain 2001
Large Print edition 2002
Harlequin Mills & Boon Limited,
Eton House, 18-24 Paradise Road,
Richmond, Surrey TW9 1SR*

© Meredith Webber 2001

ISBN 0 263 17169 8

*Set in Times Roman 16½ on 17½ pt.
17-0402-52883*

*Printed and bound in Great Britain
by Antony Rowe Ltd, Chippenham, Wiltshire*

CHAPTER ONE

'THAT'S it, I'm through with him. What does he think I am, an idiot? The first time we arrange to have what could be called a real date, and he cancels it.'

Phoebe slammed out of Charles Marlowe's office and ran straight into the arms of his senior associate.

Nick David steadied her, his hands resting lightly on her shoulders as she struggled to regain her footing.

He looked down into fury-sparked dark eyes and grinned.

'I've been wondering when the worm would turn. When he'd finally goad you into showing your true colours.'

A new rage kindled more sparks as she switched the focus of her anger from Charles to him. She wrenched herself away from his supporting hands, and her clenched fists suggested she was battling an urge to do him physical harm.

5

'What do you mean, goad me into showing my true colours? What true colours?'

Nick chuckled at her indignation.

'All that ''yes, Charles, no, Charles, three bags full, Charles''! You've never shown half as much deference to me, or hesitated to tell me exactly what you thought of me, even though, I might point out, I'm your actual boss.'

'I did not—' Phoebe began, then, with the innate honesty he admired in her, added, 'Well, only when you made that poor young temporary typist fall hopelessly in love with you, then roared at her when she couldn't do her work because of heart palpitations.'

She turned away after delivering this excuse, heading for the cupboard-like space they used as a tearoom. Nick followed, ready to argue, but when he entered the room, and had nodded in answer to coffee she'd offered by waving the jar towards him, another angle to the conversation struck him.

'You mentioned this supposed power of mine over females. If it's so potent, so all-conquering, how come you fell for Charles and not me?'

She busied herself with the coffee, her back turned to him but answering casually over her shoulder, 'I was immunised against men like you at an early age. And I did not ''fall'' for Charles, as you so crudely put it. If you remember, he was going through a bad time when I first came to work here. I felt sorry for him. Then I was attracted to his good qualities.'

Nick's huff of mocking disbelief made her swing around.

'Anyway, that's not the point,' she added, waving the teaspoon like a weapon in front of her. 'It's over, finished, kaput! In fact, I told him I'm going to go out and say yes to the first man I meet. Yes to a date—to anything he asks!'

'Now, there's a challenge, Dr Moreton,' Nick said, thinking he should make Phoebe angry more often, as the heightened colour in her cheeks and the sparks in her eyes brought her rather quiet beauty to brilliant life.

'What do you mean?' she demanded, spooning sugar into his coffee then stirring it.

'Well, I'm the man!' he said, and when she looked bewildered he explained. 'The first man you met after you told him off. That's me.' He smiled at her, and pretended to look deeply thoughtful. 'Now, what would I like you to say yes to?'

A tremor, which might have been presentiment, ran through Phoebe's body.

Or maybe she was getting a chill.

'Don't be silly,' she told Nick. 'I didn't mean it literally. But from time to time, men do ask me out, you know, and all this time I've said no, because I really thought Charles and I might have had something going for us.'

A sadness swept across her. She'd been sure they had something going for them. Or would have had. Eventually...

She knew he was dedicated to his work, which didn't give him much time for a social life, but Charles was so exactly the kind of man she'd always dreamed of marrying.

Steady, focussed, undemanding...

Everything her father wasn't?

She tried to ignore the unspoken question but she didn't need a psychologist to tell her why she'd avoided relationships—or eventually been drawn to a man like Charles.

'Hey! It's not so bad,' Nick said, coming closer and taking her chin in his hand, tilting her head up so she had to look into his eyes.

Blue, but not the soft, powdery blue of Charles's eyes. A deeper colour, with green added—hard to read.

Especially now.

You're immune to men like him, she reminded herself, then realised she'd missed what he was saying.

'What was that?' she queried, when a mental replay of what she must have heard made her move away from him again.

He picked up his coffee before he replied, and bent his head to sip it so she couldn't see the expression on his face.

'I said it mightn't be a bad idea. Perhaps what he needs is to see you with someone else. He doesn't seem to realise how unfair he's being to you, so if it looks as if you're enjoying another man's company, he might wake up.'

'Make him jealous, you mean?' Phoebe said, feeling a frown tugging her eyebrows together as she tried to imagine such an unlikely occurrence. 'But Charles isn't the jealous type. I mean, half the trouble in our relationship— if you could call a handful of dates and occasional meals after work a relationship—is because he worries so much about Anne. He worries about the unreliable men she keeps going out with, and about her being hurt by them.'

Nick rolled his eyes in disbelief. Could women really fall for the line men like Charles fed them? Not that he wanted to be the one to disillusion Phoebe. If she was genuinely in love with Charles, pointing out his faults wasn't going to do any good.

'You could try it,' he suggested. 'Better than sitting around the place, moping and pining.'

'You're right!' For a moment she looked almost cheerful, then the face that was usually so serenely lovely creased into uncertainty and she gave a despairing sigh. 'But it won't work. I mean, Charles is always here in the unit, or at home writing articles, or chasing after Anne to sort out her problems. Our entire social life has consisted of shared evenings in the lab and an occasional movie or drink on the way home from work. He wouldn't notice if I was dating ten other men, unless I had them running in and out of the rooms, or meeting me at the front door with flowers and chocolates.'

'I think ten might be overdoing it,' Nick said mildly, though mild didn't exactly describe his reaction to the thought. It had been bad enough watching the offhand way Charles had treated Phoebe, without seeing her playing up to a bevy of admirers. Not that his concern was personal. It was merely because, as a junior employee in the unit he headed, he felt some responsibility for her. 'Anyway, the answer's far closer to home. We come back to your threat. The first man you met as you slammed out of his office. Me.'

He could see the suspicion in her eyes, and feel it in a sudden tension in the room.

'You?'

'I *am* a man,' he pointed out, part amused and part peeved by her reaction.

'But you only date blondes. Charles would know straight away it was a set-up.'

Nick was surprised by the spurt of anger this blunt statement provoked. Anger that sought physical relief—like shaking the infuriating woman he was trying to help.

Not that he hadn't felt like shaking her any number of times over the past few months. Gently, of course, and perhaps more metaphorically than practically. Anything to get her to see Charles as he really was—a man who found it impossible to cut the ties with his ex-wife, no matter how lovely a new love interest might be. Jess had found that out.

However, now wasn't the time to point this out to his junior colleague. Or mention Jess.

'I have been known to take out the odd red-head,' he protested. 'And a sultry brunette or two has graced my presence in the past.'

Phoebe snorted—a most unladylike sound given the general demeanour of poise and gentility she usually displayed.

'What about Olivia, or is it Ophelia, who's the flavour of the week this week? What do you intend to tell her?'

'Juliet—' he put a special emphasis on the name, which he was sure Phoebe knew quite well '—found she preferred solicitors to doctors after all. She's moved on.'

'Or was pushed?' his offsider said, with a smile so pert and knowing it brought physical violence back to mind.

He curbed the urge.

'At any rate, she'll pose no problem.' He glanced at his watch. 'But shouldn't we be taking advantage of Charles's imminent departure, rather than arguing?'

He lifted the coffee cup from Phoebe's fingers and set it on the bench, then, holding her by the arm, he marched her out into the corridor.

Phoebe felt a flutter of uncertainty. It was OK to tease Nick about his women, and to exchange barbed banter with him when she had Charles as a secure back-stop, but these were unchartered waters, and she knew, with an inner certainty deeper than instinct, that sharks would be the least of her worries.

'What are you doing? We doing?' she demanded, as Nick positioned her against the wall, placing her with the care he usually reserved for patients.

'You're saying yes to the first man who asked you, sweetheart,' he murmured, his blue eyes aglint with wicked delight. 'Just the moment we hear the doorknob turn.'

She had barely assimilated the words, let alone grasped their meaning, when the rattle of the doorknob suggested Charles was about to leave his office.

Before she could protest, Nick lowered his head, and the lips she'd often fantasised about—only because they were so well shaped, not because she'd hankered for his kisses—claimed hers.

And 'claimed' was the correct word. There was nothing gentle about this mock embrace. The pressure was relentless, forcing her to open her own lips, demanding her tongue touch his, drawing from her a response so fevered she forgot why they were doing it.

Ripples of sensation spread downward to other parts of her body, building and building until the trickle became a flood of totally new inner awareness. It sought out secret parts and sparked them to life, contracting muscles to an aching tightness and causing a jittery alertness in her nerves.

Pleasant or unpleasant? Different, certainly. Quite possibly addictive. She wanted to stop so she could analyse this new phenomenon, but didn't want to stop in case it disappeared and was lost for ever.

Heat fogged her mind and she gave in to the new sensations, revelling in this strange awakening of a physical self she barely knew.

Until Charles's voice—his shocked, 'Phoebe!'—penetrated the bright haze surrounding her and she struggled to escape Nick's imprisoning arms.

'Remember it's all in a good cause,' he murmured against her skin, the warmth of his breath making her tingle all the way down to her toes.

A good cause, she repeated weakly to herself, then she sank beneath the waves again, kissing Nick with all the fervour of an explorer intent on discovering new lands.

Footsteps echoed down the corridor, somewhere a door was shutting, but the noises were peripheral, meaning nothing, as Phoebe gave in to an excitement she'd never felt before— hadn't realised existed.

In the end, it stopped as suddenly as it had started, Nick breaking the contact, leaning back against the wall beside her and mopping his brow with the back of his hand—an extravagant gesture supported by his hearty, 'Phew!'

Phoebe wanted to object to this theatrical reaction, but breathing was difficult enough without trying to form words, so it was Nick who spoke first.

'Talk about still waters,' he muttered, squinting suspiciously at her from his position against the wall. 'If you've been kissing poor old Charles like that, no wonder the guy's confused.'

Before she had time to tell him she'd never kissed Charles, or anyone else for that matter, with the wanton abandon she'd so recently displayed, he pushed himself upright and walked away. When he reached the door leading into his office, he opened it, then turned back towards her.

'OK,' he said, his voice so calm she realised he'd almost certainly exaggerated the kiss-reaction, 'what shall we do for an encore?'

She should have told him right then there'd be no encore. Been firm about it, as the whole idea was too ridiculous to contemplate. But the words wouldn't come. Wouldn't even take shape in her head. It was as if the kiss had short-circuited her thought processes, hot-wired her brain so it had crashed like an over-extended computer hard drive.

'Obviously kissing in the corridor has its limits,' Nick continued in such a calm, reasonable tone he might have been discussing the roster. 'How about the hospital ball? Isn't it on in a fortnight? Charles will be there for sure—he never misses official functions. Shall we make it a date?'

Phoebe knew she had to react, so she shook her head. She was going to the ball with Charles.

Or was she?

She nodded, then realised her mistake when Nick said, 'Great!' He disappeared into his office, closing the door on any further conversation.

She'd see him tomorrow. Tell him she couldn't go with him.

Although Charles would certainly go, with or without a partner, and she had her own ticket...

Phoebe detached herself from the wall and walked slowly back towards the locker room, another cupboard-like space in a small unit where the maximum floor area had been given over to consulting rooms, laboratory, storage of essential equipment and providing what patient comfort they could.

Changing into street clothes might help restore her equilibrium, although she doubted whether anything short of a brain transplant would erase the memory of that kiss.

CHAPTER TWO

THE skin cancer clinic of the dermatology department at Southern Cross Hospital was housed at the back of the long, low building, with direct access from the parking area for the many outpatients they saw. Phoebe had come in that way every morning for the past six months, always with a feeling of pleasurable satisfaction that she'd not only qualified as a doctor, a profession which held continuous satisfaction for her, but had also been offered a job in the clinic.

In the past, of course, there'd been an added element of pleasure—seeing Charles each day, working with him, sharing the challenges of front-line skin-cancer treatment and research.

Today, there was nothing but foreboding. It lay heavy in her heart, and weighed down her feet, making her knees ache with an unwillingness to carry her forward.

'Come on! Where's the woman who positively dances through these doors each morning?'

Nick came up behind her and, with an arm around her waist, urged her forward.

'It's all very well for you,' she snapped at him, straightening her legs to stop the momentum then stumbling when his pressure didn't ease. 'Everyone knows your reputation with women. You can get away with anything. But what about me? How am *I* going to face him?'

'As you always do,' Nick told her. 'With a bright smile and a cheery ''good morning, Charles''. After all, you're trying to make the man sit up and take notice. Caving in at this stage isn't going to get you anywhere.'

It took a minute for her to assimilate this, as Nick's arm around her waist was regenerating the heat and jittery nerves, reminding her of the feel of his body against hers. Of The Kiss!

The memories were distracting to say the least.

She was moving reluctantly forward when Nick spoke again.

'In fact, given the aim of the exercise, do you think another kiss might be in order? Charles has just driven into the car park. You must have rattled him last night. It's not like him to be the last arrival.'

'He probably had to visit Anne on his way,' Phoebe said, then wondered why she didn't feel the usual pang of annoyance associated with such a thought.

Was it the false security of Nick's arm around her waist, or the way he was dropping little kisses on her temple?

Totally meaningless, of course. He was probably watching Charles out of the corner of his eye as he did it, and taking great delight in taunting his colleague.

Which wasn't entirely fair and she should resist, but her body, perhaps as a result of the short-circuiting the previous afternoon, wasn't responding to the move-away messages her brain was sending it.

'I thought you had a very important meeting with a potential donor this morning,' Charles snapped at Nick as he drew closer.

'Not till ten-thirty,' Nick said calmly. 'Though I guess we should be moving, sweet-heart.'

Charles winced at the endearment and sent Phoebe, who had by this time extricated herself from Nick's clasp, a frown of utter contempt.

It's your fault, she wanted to say, but she knew it wasn't—not entirely. Charles had cancelled arrangements they'd made to eat together after work, usually to rush off to Anne's assistance, but when he was with her he'd acted like a perfect gentleman.

Too perfect?

Was that why he continued to take such responsibility for Anne?

'Good morning, Charles,' she said, parroting the words Nick had suggested she say. She smiled brightly in Charles's direction but couldn't meet his eyes, then, with legs suddenly willing to carry her anywhere as long as it was away from these two men, she strode briskly into the lobby. She nodded at the security guard and flashed her ID at him, then dashed down the corridor to their suite of rooms.

With any luck, Nick and Charles would both go into their offices where Sheree, their shared secretary, would have a pile of work waiting for each of them.

Phoebe slipped off her light linen jacket, exchanging it for a freshly laundered white coat, combed the chin-length dark hair Nick's embrace had mussed, then entered the bigger of the two consulting rooms where their camera and computerised equipment were set up. Joanne, their regular nurse, was on leave, and there was no sign of her replacement, a grumpy female who had made it obvious she thought skin was a very unexciting organ. Eight pounds and eighteen square feet of boredom! That was her outspoken opinion of skin.

Phoebe sighed. Sheree had doubtless alerted the nursing supervisor to this problem, but until a replacement arrived, and possibly even then, the task of explaining to patients what they were about to do would fall to her.

Mrs Dixon was already waiting, right on time for her six-monthly check. Phoebe brought her through to the examination room.

'No need to tell me about it, ducks,' she said cheerfully. 'The doctors here have been taking pictures of my lumps and bumps for years now. I'll take off my clothes, shall I?'

'Now, there's a suggestion I rarely hear from a good-looking woman,' a deep voice said, and Phoebe shivered, though their patient chuckled at Nick's cheeky remark.

'Go on with you,' the older woman said, then she smiled at Phoebe. 'Dr David and I are old friends. Ever since he found a melanoma on my leg five years ago, he's been taking these nude pictures of me.'

'A superficial spreading melanoma,' Nick explained for Phoebe's benefit.

'You caught it before it became nodular, then?' she asked, knowing from her study that the flat, slow-spreading plaque only became dangerous once it bulged into a raised lump.

'We did,' Nick confirmed, his back to both women now as he checked the video camera and the cable linking it to the computer.

While Mrs Dixon slipped behind the screen to change into a loose cotton gown, Phoebe studied that back.

Clad like her in a short white coat, it could be the back of any doctor in the hospital, she told herself, but she knew it was a lie. Charles was a well-built man, but not even he had shoulders as broad as Nick's, or a definite taper from them towards his hips—lean hips, she knew, although today their definition was hidden by the coat.

She was immune to men like Nick, she reminded herself, and dragged her attention back to work-related matters.

'Is Mrs Dixon part of the research group?' she asked.

'From the beginning,' Nick replied, turning from the computer to smile at her, before pressing the button to start filming. Phoebe saw her own image appear on the screen, but it wasn't enough to distract her from her surreptitious examination of Nick.

When he'd smiled, tiny lines had fanned out at the corners of his eyes. How come she'd never noticed them before?

'Ready for me?' Mrs Dixon asked, shuffling forward in the paper slippers the hospital supplied, then stopping on the mark on the floor where she obviously knew she'd be in focus for the camera.

Phoebe stepped towards the camera. It was her job to operate it, allowing it to sweep across Mrs Dixon's body, while the woman, her coat removed, rotated very slowly, holding her hands above her head when asked.

'No. I'll work the camera,' Nick said. 'You study the images on the screen. See if you can bring up the most recent test in a different colour so we get a colour mix where there's been no change, and a rim of new colour if any marks or imperfections have increased in size. Alert me to anything different.'

This was a step up from operating the camera, Phoebe knew, and her pleasure in being trusted to do it was only slightly outweighed by a new uneasiness she was feeling in Nick's presence.

She reminded herself again of her immunity and sat down at the computer, using a split screen to show the last of the series of pictures on Mrs Dixon's file alongside the ones Nick was taking now.

'Got the full-frontal shot up on screen?' he asked, and she nodded.

'Now focus in on the upper chest and neck area.'

Phoebe pressed the zoom command which magnified the picture Nick wanted, then tapped the sequence of buttons which allowed the program to merge the old and new images.

'No rims of clear colour,' she confirmed, but he must have turned from the camera and stepped closer because his hand rested lightly on her shoulder and the heat of his body warmed her back as he leant over to study the screen.

He fiddled with the colour definition, then he was gone, telling her which angle to bring up next. It was work as usual, she told herself, and as he obviously wasn't suffering body tremors from that fleeting contact, she'd better get over this new nervousness and on with the job.

'This is the last. Back view and merge,' Nick said.

'What's this merge you're talking about?' Mrs Dixon asked.

'We're trying to develop a new computer program,' Nick explained, 'which I hope will be able to show even the smallest of changes in shape or texture of a mole or other skin discoloration.'

'Can't you do that by just looking at it?' his patient demanded. 'What about the pictures my GP takes?'

'You're a nosy woman, aren't you?' Nick teased, and Phoebe heard the woman chuckle.

'I like to know things,' Mrs Dixon explained.

'And so you should,' Nick told her. 'But right now I have to go and beg some money from a possible benefactor so we can keep playing with the camera and computer program. Phoebe will tell you all about it as she does the physical examination.'

He leant over Phoebe once again to study the screen, reminded her to save everything, then touched her lightly on the shoulder before walking swiftly out of the room.

'He's a lovely man!' Mrs Dixon remarked as the door shut behind Nick.

Not wanting to say the jury was still out as far as she was concerned, Phoebe nodded and changed the subject.

'You were asking about the video images,' she reminded the patient. 'The photos your GP takes are scanned into a computer and compared, using a specially designed computer program to detect any changes. This is an aid to the general practitioner who doesn't have a lot of technical equipment in his office. All he needs is a scanner and a computer.'

She put on the tiny magnifying glasses she used for physical examination of the skin and slowly circled the still naked woman.

'I don't know much technical stuff,' her patient said. 'What's a scanner?'

Phoebe explained how the machine transferred the image to the computer hard drive.

'Once it's in the computer, the old and new photos can be brought up on the screen and compared.'

'The doctor could have done that by putting the two photos on the desk and looking at them there,' Mrs Dixon told her, scurrying back behind the screen now Phoebe had indicated she was finished.

'Yes, and measured them and noted any changes. The computer program will cut down on time, and presumably will be more accurate in its assessment. I mean, you can look at a photo of a brown mole for a long time, wondering if it's got darker or not, whereas the computer can measure the depth of colour and tell you straight away.'

'So why the video? Why do I have to come all the way into town to see you people if my local doctor can do all this?'

Phoebe chuckled at the older woman's persistence.

'You're coming into town to help the team develop a new program that will make things even easier for your local doctor. As you know from your own experience, the earlier we can detect skin cancers, the better chance the patient has of a full recovery. If the video idea works, a local GP with this technology will be able to detect changes much more easily.'

'But the patient has to go to him first,' Mrs Dixon reminded her.

'Exactly!' Phoebe agreed. 'That's one of the reasons Nick's trying to get sponsorship for the clinic from big business firms. The next stage would be using the images for early detection without a comparison with an earlier photo, but even now the video and computer could be set up in a small caravan—in a number of small caravans—and tour the state at regular intervals, in much the same way mammograms and blood collection are done in suburban and country areas.'

'The van could go to the beaches in summer,' Mrs Dixon suggested. 'You can tell young people about protecting their skin until you're blue in the face, but does it get through?'

She collected her handbag, thanked Phoebe politely and walked away, leaving Phoebe to return to the screen where the images were still displayed.

She filed them carefully, then quit the file, bringing up the next patient on the day's list. Ryan Abrams, thirty, in remission after treatment for a malignant melanoma. Maybe Mrs Dixon was right about young people not listening. The danger of too much exposure to the sun had been known for thirty years, yet Mr Abrams was only one of many patients in the 'young' bracket.

'Young, male and stupid!' Charles said, much later, when the three of them had gathered in Nick's office in response to Phoebe's request that they discuss Mr Abrams's case. 'They're in the highest risk bracket these days.'

'You can't blame young men for thinking a shady hat, a long-sleeved shirt and a slathering of sunscreen isn't quite the macho image they're trying to project,' Nick reminded him.

'We need a covered-up cult hero to impress them,' Phoebe suggested.

'I can't quite picture a rock guitarist in long sleeves, sunglasses and a hat.' Nick raised a lazy eyebrow as he turned towards her, and she saw the glint of amusement in his eyes.

You're immune, she reminded herself as that teasing glance from blue-green depths sent erratic impulses along her nerves.

'I'll show you the images,' she said, diverting the conversation back to work while mentally reminding herself of Nick's similarity to her father.

Her much-married father!

She shifted to the chair in front of the computer and brought up the section of skin she wanted to show the specialists, then enlarged the discoloured lesion.

'I took Polaroid shots as well,' she added, spinning in the chair so she faced the two men and fanning the photos out across the desk.

'But that's—' Charles began

'What do you think it is, Phoebe?' Nick asked, silencing Charles with a wave of his hand.

'It's described on his file as a blue nevi—'

'A mole which has no malignant potential. Many young adults develop them,' Charles reminded her, projecting such profound disdain into his voice that she shifted uncomfortably in her seat.

'I know, but as far as I've been able to discover, they don't change colour, and this one is definitely darker than it was on Mr Abrams's visit a month ago.'

Nick stood up and crossed to where she sat, bending over her to study the computer screen.

'Have you printed out a colour density comparison?' he asked, his head so close she could

see every movement of the lips which had
caused such chaos the previous afternoon.

'That's what's bothering me,' she told
him—although it wasn't all that was bothering
her. Nick's closeness was affecting her skin,
making it prickle with an awareness he'd never
before generated.

She took a deep breath and explained. 'The
program doesn't seem to recognise a difference in the density, although to the naked eye,
as well as on the screen and on the prints,
there's a distinct difference. I did a merge, and
the size and shape haven't altered.'

'If the computer doesn't recognise a colour
change, it doesn't exist,' said Charles, joining
Nick behind her chair and speaking with the
authority of the man who had fine-tuned the
computer program.

He rested his hand on Phoebe's shoulder in
such a proprietorial manner that she had to resist an urge to shrug it off.

'Mr Abrams—Ryan, isn't he?' Nick said, in
a voice that suggested he was trying to place
him. 'Young, fair-haired, grey eyes…'

'Panicky chap,' Charles added, as Nick
tapped the keys to bring the patient's personal
details up on the screen.

'I'd be panicky if I were diagnosed with a malignant tumour when I was twenty-six,' he said. 'Ah, yes. Ryan Abrams! Doesn't he usually see you, Charles?'

'It was a routine visit. One that Phoebe can easily handle.'

'I'm not saying she can't,' Nick said, and now Phoebe had two hands on her shoulders. One on each side—one from each man! Only Nick's was holding her still, stalling a protest. 'But our Mr Abrams once tried a similar trick with me when you were on leave. He painted a pale tan dye around a mole, creating an irregular edge so it gave the impression of a halo developing around a melanoma. Fortunately for him, I wiped the dye off when I swabbed the skin prior to excising it. I'd say he's used ink or the tip of a felt pen this time, so the colour has changed.'

'But why wouldn't the computer pick it up?' Phoebe asked as Charles spun away.

His voice revealed a natural aggravation as he muttered, 'Does he think this is funny?'

'The computer picks up density which in the natural progression of malignancy comes from a proliferation of cells. It wouldn't see cell proliferation here, so ignored it.' Nick answered

Phoebe first then straightened up and turned to Charles.

'I don't think he does it as a joke, although he may pretend that's what it is when we put it to him.' He paused, then added. 'I think you're right about him being panicky. He's terrified that if he does get another suspicious lesion, we won't notice it. He's testing us—testing our methods and equipment.'

'He's wasting our time,' Charles said angrily.

'And his,' Nick reminded him. 'You did tell him it would probably require excision, didn't you Phoebe?'

She nodded.

'I'd have got Charles to do it then and there, but he was up on the ward, so Mr Abrams is coming back early tomorrow.'

She picked up the photographs and studied them.

'I hope that's all it is,' she said quietly, and once again Nick's hand rested lightly on her shoulder.

'So do we all,' he said, though the glare Charles shot them both suggested that he didn't wish to be included in the 'all'.

CHAPTER THREE

NICK saw the worried look in Phoebe's eyes as she watched Charles disappear through the door, and knew her soft heart was prompting a confession. Personally, he was only too anxious to cause Charles some grief. The man had gone on and on at him this morning, making it sound as if Nick had seduced Phoebe in the corridor, rather than just kissing her.

'I should explain to him—tell him the kiss was just a joke,' she said, right on cue.

'Is that all it was?' Nick asked, while telling himself he'd better believe it. Phoebe wasn't the kind of woman he sought out for company—she was far too young, too trusting, for someone like him. He preferred women who were looking for a good time rather than a steady relationship. At the moment work took preference over any relationship, and as for commitment—the word brought with it such burdens, such family obligations, he didn't want to think about it.

As for Phoebe, she might be a fully qualified medical practitioner, but she'd somehow emerged from her years of study and hospital work with an innocence at odds with her twenty-five years.

An innocence which aroused all his protective instincts.

'Weren't you intending to make him jealous? Do you think that will work if you cave in after one cool look and a couple of angry glares?'

She looked at him and frowned, giving her face a look of such adorable uncertainty he was almost impelled to kiss her again.

Reassuringly, of course.

Only he hadn't quite figured out his reaction to the previous kiss, so kissing her again definitely wasn't on the agenda.

'I don't think I can play that kind of game,' she said, shifting her shoulders as if her skin were suddenly too tight. 'It's like Mr Abrams and the false alarms.'

Nick considered the alternative, which was seeing Phoebe unhappy because Charles, once reassured of her continued loyalty, would again neglect her for Anne. Nick reminded himself he'd already been through that with

Jess, another soft-hearted woman who'd fallen for Charles's pathetic 'poor me' act.

Now that he considered it, he hated seeing Phoebe unhappy.

'Is it?' he asked. 'I'd have thought it was more like asserting yourself. Or perhaps self-preservation. It's not as if you haven't given Charles time to draw a line under his relationship with Anne and make a commitment to one with you.'

Phoebe hesitated, then her lips widened into a smile.

'You're right! I'm weak, that's all. I hate seeing him look so unhappy.'

'Now, that I do understand,' Nick told her as her words echoed his thoughts about her. Thank heavens she wouldn't guess exactly what he meant. 'So, let's sit down and plan our campaign. On Friday evening—heavens, that's the day after tomorrow—Charles and I, among others, are having dinner with a couple of skin specialists visiting from the States. Had Charles mentioned it to you?'

Phoebe opened her mouth to say that Charles never invited her to what he termed 'business' dinners then decided that would be disloyal. She made do with a negative shake of her head, though as Nick seemed to think it natural to take a woman, why hadn't Charles ever asked her?

'Is that vacant look a yes?' Nick asked.

'Vacant look? What needs a yes?'

He sighed.

'My invitation to join us for dinner on Friday night. You'll come?'

He spoke as he did when checking through her work schedule. Which was how it should be, she reminded herself.

'Yes,' she said. 'What time Friday and where?'

Nick looked affronted.

'I'll pick you up at your place,' he said. 'Seven or seven-thirty depending on how late we get away from work. I've booked a table at Printemps, so it will be good casual, not dressy.'

Phoebe smiled to herself. Trust a lady's man like Nick to cover the essentials.

'Then next week,' he continued, obviously caught up in 'the plan', 'we'll have to try to co-ordinate our lunch hours so we can sit to-gether. Then a week on Saturday, we've got the ball.'

The confusion she'd felt when he'd first mentioned the ball returned—a hundredfold.

'I don't know about the ball,' she began, trying to choose her words with care. After all, Nick was only doing this for her and she didn't want to hurt his feelings. 'As far as I could gather when I did my intern year here at Southern Cross, it's the main hospital function of the year, and any couple seen at it together are linked for ever.'

Nick's grin caused a slight queasiness in her stomach.

'Scared of being linked to me for ever?' he teased.

'Terrified' would have been a better word, but she didn't utter her thoughts and he added, 'Anyway, those assumptions don't apply to me. In fact, I make sure of it by squiring a different beauty every year.'

'Why?'

She hadn't meant to ask, but when the word popped out and she saw the gleams of laughter disappear from his eyes, she knew she wanted an answer.

'Safety in numbers?' he said lightly.

'Or scared of commitment?' she countered, although common sense told her not to pry.

'Terrified,' he said, standing up and touching her lightly on the shoulder, signalling an end to the conversation.

He'd spoken the word she hadn't used earlier and she guessed, although he'd smiled as he said it, there was an underlying truth behind it.

'Strong word, Nick,' she said, not exactly prying but interested enough to ignore his signal.

'Not strong enough, if you knew my mother and her crazy beliefs about the sanctity of marriage—or perhaps the longevity of it would be a better way of putting it. Talk about putting pressure on a man! That and the demands of work make me a poor marriage prospect.'

He moved away and she took the hint this time, guessing he wouldn't answer any more questions.

Not that she could probe any deeper. Any relationship between them was pretence.

'So, as we're now back on track with the plan, how about dinner?' He shifted the conversation with the skill of a diplomat. 'I've a meeting at eight, but we could grab a quick bite in the cafeteria if you're not committed to going home. Charles will be in the cafeteria for sure. Eating there before the same meeting.'

He'd expected support for this excellent suggestion but Phoebe was frowning again.

'You don't have to do this, you know,' she said. 'I mean, making him jealous—it was a fairly juvenile idea. I could just not see him— make it plain the relationship, if an occasional date could be called such a thing, is over.'

Nick put out his forefinger and smoothed the worry lines away.

'You should know me well enough by now to know I rarely do anything I don't want to do. And as the making-him-jealous idea was mine, I'd like to refute the ''juvenile'' suggestion. He's been taking you for granted, Phoebe, and if we have to make him a little uncomfortable in order for him to realise that, then so be it.'

But he could tell she wasn't convinced.

'You have to eat,' he added persuasively, when he realised he wanted—for reasons he could not quite pin down but suspected had nothing to do with Charles—to eat with Phoebe. 'Since they upped the budget in the catering department, the cafeteria food's not bad.'

Phoebe studied his face for a moment, trying to see beyond the outer image, trying to figure out his motivation in all of this.

But the skin, a tawny gold, drawn taut over strong bones, distracted her, and the shadowy darkness where his beard would grow made her want to touch his chin, feel the roughness...

A less intense version of the sensations she'd felt the previous afternoon skittered through her body, causing a heaviness very close to pain in her breasts.

Why would simply looking at him do this?

'I don't bite,' he murmured, as if he'd felt the intensity of her gaze as she sought an answer to the strange sensations.

'That possibility wasn't my concern,' she told him, and smiled with relief because the temptation to touch had been resisted.

'Dinner?' he repeated, answering her smile with a tempting one of his own.

She shrugged.

'I guess so.'

Nick's smile disappeared, replaced by the beginnings of a frown.

'Try not to sound too enthusiastic!' he scolded. 'It might go to my head!'

She chuckled at his reaction. 'I'll do my best not to praise you too much,' she promised, relieved to be bickering light-heartedly with him again.

This Nick she could handle.

Or could she?

The doubt arose when he took her arm in the corridor, and his body pressed against her side as he steered them through the streams of patients, visitors and staff cluttering this main thoroughfare through the hospital.

His touch set off quivers of new excitement along her nerves, while her body showed a dismaying tendency to press closer to his.

'What's yellow and black and very dangerous?' she asked him as an old joke from her childhood bobbed into her head.

He slowed their progress as they reached the cafeteria door, and looked down at her with puzzled eyes.

'I give up.'

She pulled away, and pushed through the door ahead of him.

'Shark-infested custard,' she said, flinging the answer over her shoulder, then smiling as she heard his shout of laughter.

But she knew she shouldn't be smiling, no matter how comfortable the arm he slipped around her shoulders felt. The dangers of shark-infested custard didn't begin to compare with the dangers of tawny skin, dark beard shadows and blue-green eyes, all part of the package of the man whose lightest touch was sending unfamiliar tremors of sensation through her body.

'Good joke, was it?' Charles appeared from nowhere, reminding Phoebe that the arm around her shoulders was window-dressing—there to sell an idea.

'A pathetic one, actually,' she said to Charles. If Nick could put himself out to help her in this way, the least she could do was play along. She snuggled closer to the danger and added, 'But it got a laugh.'

'Have you eaten?'

Nick asked the question, and Charles, who'd obviously been leaving the room as they entered, hesitated for a moment, then said, 'Actually, yes, but I'll join you for coffee.'

He moved closer to Phoebe, who'd decided that snuggling closer to Nick wasn't a good idea and had extricated herself from his side.

'Great,' Nick responded, speaking to Charles but catching Phoebe's arm before she could escape too far. 'Why don't you grab us a table and I'll get your coffee? Long black?'

Phoebe caught a flash of anger in Charles's eyes. He knew he'd been outmanoeuvred, and he wasn't happy about it.

'Maybe we're overdoing it?' she suggested tentatively to Nick as he ushered her into the queue then stood protectively behind her.

'Don't start feeling sorry for him again,' he growled, clamping a hand on her shoulder as if he wanted to shake some sense into her.

The nerve endings in the skin beneath that hand, undeterred by several layers of fine linen, did their reacting thing again, and feeling sorry for Charles became the least of her problems.

Nick could feel her tension—a tightness in her muscles—through her clothes. It caused knots in his own stomach and he cursed Charles for hurting her like this, and inadvertently embroiling him in the mess.

Although his involvement was hardly Charles's fault, Nick admitted to himself. The 'making Charles sit up and take notice' idea was all his own folly.

Because it bothered him to see Phoebe so upset.

And to see Charles take advantage of her good nature—again and again and again.

He looked down at her as they shuffled forward towards the service counter. At what he could see of her. Glossy dark brown hair so thick a man could lose his fingers in its mass. It fascinated him—that hair. Had held his attention the day she'd come for an interview.

Or had distracted him when he'd realised he'd been staring at her face, reminded of a painting he'd once seen of a dark-haired Madonna. The woman in the painting had been so relaxed, so calm, he'd wanted to reach out and touch her, certain such serenity could restore order to his frenetic life.

They'd been dangerous thoughts for a man who wasn't in the market for a serious relationship. So dangerous, in fact, he'd been relieved when she'd shown an interest in Charles.

'Nick! Where have you been? I've been phoning you and leaving messages on your machine ever since I got back.'

He turned to the newcomer with startled dismay. Though pleased to be diverted from dis-

turbing thoughts and mental images of Phoebe
and Madonnas, the last person he'd expected
to see was Charles's previous love interest.

Here was an unexpected complication!

Think about it later, he told himself as he
kissed the tall, statuesque blonde warmly on
the cheek.

'I'm sorry if I seem dazed, but it's as if I
conjured you up. I've been thinking of you
such a lot lately.'

He grinned apologetically, then pulled himself sufficiently together to add, 'My machine's been playing up. I've just installed a
new one, so anything you've left since last
night will come through. How was your trip,
Jess?'

'Great! Just fantastic! I stole a couple of
weeks' leave and skied in the Rockies. It was
unbelievable.'

She was talking to Nick but eyeing Phoebe
with more than a passing interest. Nick remembered Phoebe's joke about shark-infested
custard, but introduced them anyway.

'Jessica Hunter, meet Phoebe Moreton, new
to our small band since you departed. Phoebe,
Jess is the computer wizard who worked with

Charles and me on the original program and gave us the clues for developing the new one.'

Jess put out her hand and explained, as Phoebe took it, 'I've been in the States on a six-month course on computer skills for use in medical technology.'

Then she looked around.

'Charles not here?'

The elaborately casual question didn't fool Nick for an instant.

'He's finding a table for us,' Phoebe said, blissfully unaware that Jess had played the role of comforter to Charles prior to her departure to the States—and Phoebe's arrival on the scene.

Or had Charles told her? Nick wondered, fancying he'd detected an element of coolness in Phoebe's voice.

'Another lovely blonde, Dr David?' she said, as Jess crossed the room towards Charles.

Definitely a coolness!

'We all worked closely together for a long time,' he said, telling himself it was for Charles's sake he was explaining.

Fortunately, they'd reached the front of the queue and Phoebe was diverted by the counter assistant.

'I'll have the roast of the day, with gravy, two potatoes, pumpkin, cauliflower and beans,' she said, amusing Nick with the decisiveness of her order. He leaned forward and murmured in her ear.

'I'm pleased to see the glitch in your love life isn't putting you off your food.'

She chuckled at the joke against herself, and admitted ruefully, 'I doubt you could call it a ''love'' life,' she said, emphasising the word 'love'. 'Although I did keep hoping it might develop that way.' She sighed, and returned to the conversation. 'Not that I can imagine anything putting me off my food. I'd never make a model—couldn't hack the dieting. I'm quite resigned to being one of those women described as having a fuller figure.'

Phoebe took her plate with a smile of thanks to the staff member and moved on, giving Nick the opportunity to study the back view of the denigrated figure.

Not reed thin, certainly, but there was nothing wrong with a neat waist swelling out to beautifully proportioned hips. Or with a bottom sweetly curved to fit right into the palms of a man's hands—

'If you're not eating, move along so I can serve someone else.'

The assistant's terse remark brought him out of thoughts he shouldn't have been having.

'I'll have what she had,' he said hastily, nodding towards Phoebe who was peering into the dessert cabinet with the air of a woman intent on her choice.

'One of each?' he suggested, when he had received his own filled plate and came alongside to find her still undecided.

'Don't tempt me,' she said, flashing him a conspiratorial grin. 'No! I think the cheesecake. It was conscience telling me the yoghurt and fruit would be better for me, and though I admit that's right, it's more a chocolate cheesecake kind of evening, isn't it?'

Nick nodded, which was easier than speaking, given the track his wayward mind had taken. Though this teasing light-heartedness was a side of Phoebe he didn't know. Intriguing, really. Fun...

'Put them on this tray,' he told her, as they shuffled forward again. 'Then you can collect cutlery while I get the coffee and pay.'

She obeyed the first command, but baulked at him paying.

'Of course I'll pay,' he told her, forcing her forward by advancing the tray in her direction.

'But Charles won't know whether you did or didn't, so it can't matter,' she pointed out, reaching into the pocket of her jacket and pulling out a crumpled note.

'But I want to pay,' Nick said, then was disconcerted by what sounded like petulance in his voice.

'Tough!' the woman he'd been pitying said bluntly. She spun around, reached the till and proffered her crumpled note, pointing back towards the tray and adding orders for three coffees.

At least she hadn't taken independence to the stage where she'd paid for his. He'd just registered this decidedly grumpy thought when she turned back to him.

'I paid for yours as well, as you're only doing this for me,' she said, flashing him a smile.

It was a reminder he didn't need, though how a busy, level-headed man like himself had come to be embroiled in such a quixotic undertaking, he couldn't imagine.

Oh, yes, you can, an inner voice said sternly. It was your idea! No doubt prodded by a subconscious niggle that she'd preferred Charles right from the start.

Phoebe collected cutlery and napkins then led the way to a table by the window where Charles and Jessica were sitting side by side, chatting like old friends. For a moment she wished that was how things had been. That Jessica had been Charles's girlfriend, rather than Nick's.

The thought, fleeting though it was, alarmed her but she hid her reaction behind a cheerful smile and slid into a chair opposite Charles.

Nick deposited the tray on the table, passed Charles his coffee, then set Phoebe's plate in front of her, pushing the desserts to one side while they tackled their main courses.

'Gosh, fancy being able to eat like that and not put on weight,' Jess said, and Phoebe glanced up, suspecting a barb in the words. But Jess's smile was warm and friendly, so lacking in malice that Phoebe found herself smiling back. No wonder Nick liked the woman, she thought, and was surprised by a momentary twinge of regret.

It turned into a twinge of a different kind when Nick touched her lightly on the wrist, then let his fingers linger against her skin.

He's doing it as part of the plan, she reminded herself. Or perhaps he has his own agenda—making Jessica jealous. But the warmth of that touch seared through her regardless of its genesis, reminding Phoebe that she might be playing a dangerous game.

She dragged her attention back to the conversation, which apparently concerned Mr Abrams.

'Phoebe picked it up,' Nick was telling Jess. 'But I suspect a scam rather than a computer glitch.'

'I'll take a look at it when you've finished eating,' Jess suggested. 'I was on my way out when I saw you.'

Nick glanced at his watch.

'Charles and I have a meeting at eight.' Phoebe imagined she heard regret in his voice. 'I won't have time, but Charles is finished. Maybe he and you…'

Phoebe glanced at Charles. He looked less than delighted. In fact, he looked as if he was suffering considerable strain. She should have been pleased but something told her the strain was more likely to be because of Anne's latest dilemma than her own play-acting with Nick.

Jess was already on her feet, urging Charles to finish his coffee and accompany her back to the rooms. Charles pushed the coffee to one side, looked wildly towards Nick, then stood up, ran a hand distractedly through his usually immaculate hair, and followed Jess towards the door.

'He looks rattled,' Phoebe observed, wondering why she didn't feel the slightest sense of triumph.

'So he should,' Nick told her, favouring her with a smile that jolted her heart.

How could this be? What was happening to her immunity? Why was she reacting to every facial change of Nick's and not feeling at all upset about Charles's obvious discomfort?

She concentrated on her meal though she was no longer hungry. Which was another worry, now she considered it. No matter what drama might be playing out in her life, she *never* lost her appetite.

'I'll eat the second potato if you can't manage,' Nick said, and when she nodded he leaned across and dug his fork into it, then lifted it off her plate.

A sense of intimacy in the action sent an involuntary shiver down her spine, and though she hid it by pushing her plate away and reaching for her dessert, chocolate cheesecake was the last thing she wanted to tackle.

Perhaps if she thought about work...

'Mr Abrams must be terrified of a recurrence to be playing silly games with us,' she said. 'How can you—we—reassure him? Ease his fears?'

'It's a huge problem and I'm not certain how to tackle it,' Nick admitted. 'He needs support from us, but the play-acting has to stop.'

'He hasn't many skin lesions—well, not hundreds,' Phoebe said, thinking back to the images she'd taken. 'Could we excise all of them? Would that help?'

'It's what he'd like us to do,' Nick told her. 'He's already suggested that. Why not take them all off and eliminate any chance of their turning cancerous?'

He paused and Phoebe prompted him.

'Well, why not? Aren't some women with a family history of breast cancer having radical mastectomies as a preventative measure?'

'I've heard of it happening,' Nick agreed, 'but it's not something I'd recommend with melanoma. In my opinion it could give the patient a false sense of security. Then he might not continue to come for regular checks, and could miss a new lesion—perhaps in an inaccessible place. As you know, a superficial spreading melanoma can start off quite pale. Like a layer of plaque on the skin.'

'Easy to miss,' Phoebe murmured, cutting the cheesecake into tiny pieces and pushing them around the plate. 'But if removing all his moles isn't an option, what else can we do?'

'Reassure him our screening works?' Nick shrugged as if he knew that wasn't going to be enough. 'Have him come in more regularly? Suggest counselling to help him deal with his fears?'

'Can anyone who's been through the diagnosis and treatment of a malignant melanoma ever learn to deal with their fears?'

Phoebe looked at Nick and saw her own concern mirrored on his face. Then he smiled, a tiny half smile that did little more than tilt one corner of those tantalising lips.

She ate some cheesecake, hoping a chocolate fix might restore normality to the situation.

'Perhaps counselling could give him strategies to handle them.' His left eyebrow lifted as he spoke. 'Is that phrasing it better?'

She should have looked away, but the mobility of his face, an intensity in his eyes as he leaned towards her, held her, and she nodded, mesmerised by the thought of what might happen next.

'Charles isn't here,' he murmured, 'so we'd have to consider it a rehearsal.'

The conversational switch should have startled her, but her own anticipatory feeling had been so strong she wasn't surprised to find it was mutual.

His lips brushed hers, then claimed them again, and, sitting at a table in the hospital cafeteria, with a half-eaten piece of chocolate cheesecake in front of her, she kissed him back.

In the cafeteria?

Disbelief battled desire for an instant, then lost the struggle. The myriad feelings of the previous afternoon returned, though the fire within was hotter, the tug of what could only be desire far stronger. She wanted to capture the wonder of it all, define the different sensations so she could replay them later and work out what was happening.

But once again her brain had stopped processing her thoughts—intent on reacting only to sensation.

Next thing she knew Nick had eased away from her, steadied her momentarily with a hand on her shoulder, then straightened in his chair.

'Mmm, sweet chocolate,' he whispered, while Phoebe struggled to pull herself together. For the first time in her life, she understood how apt that over-used phrase could be. The kiss had reduced her to a scattering of parts, all of which had reacted differently. Her heart, already jolted earlier, was thudding, her nerves were tingling, while deep inside her a liquid heat was scorching her flesh.

It was the kissing ruining her immunity. It had to stop. The very last thing she wanted was to fall in love with Nick. He was too like her father. He'd even admitted the idea of commitment terrified him.

She battled a confusion of thought and sensation.

'I doubt one rehearsal will be enough, but sadly I have to love and leave you,' Nick said, resting his hand lightly on the nape of her neck as he pushed back his chair and rose to his feet. 'Duty calls.'

Then he bent and brushed his lips across her hair, said something that sounded like 'losing his fingers' and departed, leaving only the echo of his footsteps and a sense of total disarray in Phoebe's body.

'I don't know about him losing his fingers, but you're definitely losing your mind,' she told herself, saying the words out loud in the hope they might have more impact on her disordered senses.

She pushed away her unfinished dessert, propped her elbows on the table, rested her chin on her hands and tried to think.

Her brain, usually sharp and incisive, seemed unwilling to tackle the problem of Nick's kisses, or the unreliability of her immunity.

She'd think about Charles—honestly! The more Nick reminded her of her father, the more she realised she'd chosen Charles because he was everything her paternal relative wasn't. Meeting Charles had been like meeting the embodiment of a dream—the kind of man she'd told herself since childhood she'd eventually marry. From there it had been easy to imagine herself falling in love with him.

Easy to make more of an occasional date and shared evenings at work than there really was?

Of course she had—though, in fairness to herself, Charles had showed enough interest to encourage her to think their friendship was moving towards a closer relationship.

In any case, now she'd faced up to her motivations, and to the fact that she'd never been in love with Charles but in love with the idea of being in love, the whole scenario of making Charles jealous was pointless and had to stop.

The thought filled her with an inexplicable dismay.

Nothing made sense any more, so she stared out across the room and tried to decide why the second kiss had been more electrifying than the first. Or had its recentness simply made it seem that way?

'May I join you?'

She turned to find the slim, blonde Jessica already pulling out the chair so recently vacated by Nick.

Probably still warm from his body, Phoebe thought with a regret she knew she shouldn't feel.

'This chap you're worried about,' Jess began. 'He's not down in the appointment book and Charles wondered what time he was coming in.'

Yesterday Phoebe might have been irritated by the woman running messages for Charles, but tonight it didn't seem to matter.

'I told him early, eight o'clock, before regular appointments start.'

'Great!' Jess replied. 'I can be there at that time. I've been fiddling around with an idea for something that patients might be able to use at home. A kind of self-examination program using shots from a digital camera. It won't work for everyone, but Mr Abrams should be computer literate and it might go some way towards allaying his fears.'

'Wow!' Phoebe muttered as the idea seized her imagination. 'But might it not also make them worse? Aren't there concerns among medical people about the home blood pressure machines which are sold commercially these days?'

'Some concern,' Jess admitted. 'But not enough to stop their use. If Mr Abrams can see it as an adjunct to his normal screening visits rather than an alternative...'

'And if we can convince him to come in and see us anytime he's worried,' Phoebe added.

'Exactly,' Jess agreed.

Phoebe smiled at her, while thinking how she'd like to get to know the other woman better. Had she gone away hoping to change Nick's views on commitment?

The thought caused such physical discomfort in Phoebe's stomach she turned her attention firmly back to the topic of conversation.

'But you said you've been working on it. It doesn't exist?'

'Not yet,' Jess told her. 'But if Mr Abrams is interested, I might treat him as a guinea pig and rig up something he can use in the meantime.'

Phoebe forgot Charles and deception, and pushed Nick David to the very furthest corner of her mind. Talking to Jess about this exciting possibility was the antidote she needed—or the booster shot, perhaps that was a better analogy.

'Have you been dating Nick long?'

The question, coming after a long and technical discussion of the use of computerised technology, jolted Phoebe.

'Nick? I'm not dating Nick,' she protested. She was about to add she'd been going out occasionally with Charles, to reassure Jess she wasn't poaching, but realised this was no longer true so kept quiet.

'But you looked so…I don't know the word I need—as if something special was sparking between you.'

'An argument most probably,' Phoebe said, anxious to dispel any doubts from Jess's mind. 'We argue all the time.'

'More than we ever did,' Jess said, and Phoebe, hearing the weight of sadness in the other woman's voice, decided the charade with Nick had to end. For Jess's sake as much as anything…

'Jessica doesn't give a damn what I do,' Nick said, when Phoebe put this idea to him the following morning.

Once again they'd met in the car park, and once again he'd—casually—slung his arm around her waist.

Aware she should shrug it off, or move away, Phoebe hesitated, but let it stay.

'You might think she's over you, but she's not,' she said stoutly, and Nick chuckled.

The deep ripple of sound flowed across her skin and whispered in her blood. She forgot what she'd been trying to say, and leaned into his body as the arm tucked her closer.

'Charles approaching from the left. What is it the pilots say—angels at ten o'clock?'

It was a light-hearted remark but it reminded Phoebe that the warm arm around her waist was a sham, and Nick's kisses merely play-acting. She stepped away from it—from him—and hurried into the building, something that felt very like disappointment dogging every step she took.

CHAPTER FOUR

MR ABRAMS arrived early, dead-heating with Jess, who had introduced herself to him in the corridor.

Charles was there to greet him with a cool and very formal handshake. He ushered him through to the smaller consulting room, where Sheree had set out extra chairs. Phoebe, following them, sensed a discomfort in Charles, but he was glancing more towards Jess than herself, so she assumed it had nothing to do with the silly act she and Nick had been putting on.

'Dr David, who is head of the clinic, will be seeing you today,' Charles explained to the patient. 'Dr Moreton you know, and Miss Hunter is a specialist in medical technology.'

'I've already introduced myself and told him to call me Jess, Charles,' Jessica said. 'If you're not staying, why don't you buzz off so I can start explaining things to Ryan?'

Phoebe saw the colour rise in Charles's cheeks and wondered whether it indicated anger or embarrassment. Whatever it was, it was more reaction than she'd ever been able to generate in the man. Then Nick came in and she found it difficult to think about Charles.

About anything but the man with whom she definitely, absolutely, unequivocally, did *not* want to become involved.

Fortunately he took over, shaking hands with Ryan Abrams, inviting him to sit, waving herself and Jess into vacant chairs, and coming bluntly to the point.

'We think you may have coloured that mole, in much the same way as you used dye around another harmless lesion some months ago.' It was Ryan Abrams's turn to flush, but before he could speak Nick continued.

'We understand you feel a need to test us— to make sure in your own mind that we know what we're doing—but we have patients waiting three months for an appointment, patients who could have a dangerous melanoma just about to spread deadly cells into underlying tissue and the bloodstream.'

'But you'd see anyone whose doctor was concerned straight away,' Mr Abrams protested.

'When possible,' Nick told him. 'When we can squeeze them in.'

'And I'm wasting your time? That's what you're saying, isn't it? But what about me? What about my time? How much would I have left if it happened again?'

Jessica moved to the chair beside him and leaned over.

'We're concerned about that as well,' she told him. 'That's why we're here.'

He thrust away the hand she'd rested on his arm and glared angrily at all of them.

'If you'd just taken them all off, all my moles or whatever else you like to call them, then none of this would have happened.'

Phoebe guessed it was as close as they were going to get to an admission.

'Taking off all your moles won't guarantee protection,' Nick told him. 'I'm sure Dr Marlowe has explained to you that seventy per cent of melanomas arise from normally pigmented skin. Only thirty per cent arise from moles.'

'Seventy per cent come from normal skin?' Their patient echoed the statistic in horrified tones, at the same time searching the bare skin on his hands—all that was immediately visible to him.

'They begin as a proliferation of melano-cytes, the pigment cells which give colour to your hair as well as your skin. A bad sunburn you may not even remember suffering as a child could have affected some of those cells, and though they might lie dormant for a long time they could suddenly start multiplying. That's why we have you in for regular checks,' Nick continued. 'You're probably clued up enough to keep check on the spots you can see, but we check all of you and do computerised comparisons.'

'Which is why I'm here,' Jess said cheer-fully. 'I'm really the brains behind the program the doctors currently use and I'd like to work with you to see if it's practical to give some patients a home program.'

Ryan Abrams turned to her, clutching at her arm like a drowning man reaching for a life-raft.

'Could you do that? Set one up for me?'

'You'd still have to come in for regular checks,' Nick warned him. 'And I still want to take a look at that blue nevi today, so why don't you strip off? I'll do a check, then you and Jessica can use my office for a chat while Phoebe and I tackle today's patients.'

She and Nick to tackle today's patients? Today was a skin clinic day when most of the patients were regulars, coming in to have old lesions checked and new ones removed. It was a clinic Charles usually ran, with Phoebe assisting and learning as she helped.

'I've swapped,' Nick said to Phoebe, as Jess ushered Ryan out the door. He seemed to be answering her, though she hadn't voiced her surprise.

She lifted a chair, intending to return it to the tearoom, but Nick took it out of her hands.

'I'll restore order. Could you check with Sheree whether we're getting a nurse replacement or not?'

His shoulder brushed against her as he turned towards the inner door, and Phoebe closed her eyes and tried to stem the responses even such an accidental touch had caused.

Perhaps if she went to visit her father.

Tonight.

Nodding her head decisively, she walked back through the waiting room, murmuring a 'good morning' to the patients collecting there, before entering Sheree's office.

No Sheree. Only Charles, bent over the filing cabinet.

'Have we lost our secretary now as well?' Phoebe asked, hoping normal conversation might dispel the discomfort she was feeling in Charles's presence.

'She's getting me a cup of coffee,' he said, without interrupting his search. 'At least someone in this unit shows me a little consideration.'

The remark was so petty—and uncalled for—it stung Phoebe into retaliation.

'*I* showed you consideration,' she fumed. 'I gave you support, and understanding, and time, Charles, which you said you needed. And for what? To be told you couldn't make a commitment! Not that I wanted a for-ever-and-ever-type commitment—not immediately. I just wanted to know if we had some kind of relationship going or not!'

He swung around at that, glaring at her and nodding towards the glass wall between the office and the waiting room.

'You're making an exhibition of yourself in front of the patients,' he said coldly. 'But, then, I guess that's no more than what's to be expected of someone who's joined the ranks of Nick's women!'

Fury boiled up like molten lava, but Phoebe clamped it down. A movement beyond the glass caught her eye. Nick must have finished removing spare chairs and had now taken on the nurse's duties, entering the waiting room to call a patient, bending to help an elderly woman out of her chair. Smiling. Lips moving as he greeted her, reassured her.

The sight of him cooled Phoebe's rage, and when Sheree came in she was able to voice the question she'd been sent to ask.

'Of course they haven't sent us a replacement,' Sheree said, apparently oblivious to the atmosphere in the room as she put a mug of coffee on the cabinet for Charles. 'There's some kind of bug laying low the nursing staff, the auxiliary staff are holding stop-work meetings and the hospital administration has always had us at the very bottom of their priority list.'

Which was why Nick was always chasing wealthy businessmen who might be interested in making a donation to the clinic.

'We'll manage,' Phoebe assured her, knowing Sheree would get worked up about lack of money if given half a chance. Then, without a

backward glance at the man she'd fancied herself falling in love with since she'd first
walked into the unit, she left the room.

She wouldn't let Charles's attitude bother
her. She'd think of the funding problem instead.

'It's because people see skin as boring,'
Nick said when she raised the funding question
later. They were grabbing a cup of coffee between patients. 'Heart surgery, brain surgery,
state-of-the-art machines to delve into the very
centre of the human body—all those things can
be made to sound exciting. All people want to
do when I show them a picture of a malignant
skin tumour is throw up.'

'But skin is so important,' Phoebe protested.
'It protects the body against germs, and tissues
from injury, provides a means of temperature
control—'

'Not to mention its use as the main organ
of sensation,' Nick added, sliding his forefinger along the underside of Phoebe's arm.
'Very sensual stuff, skin!'

She shivered, inadvertently providing an appropriate response to his statement. It had been
the first thing she'd considered, but hadn't

wanted to add it to the list, thinking he might think—

'I'll bring in the next patient,' she said, stepping towards the door as swiftly as she could manage without actually running.

But what little protection she'd managed to erect around herself had vanished with that touch, and working with Nick, bending over a patient's leg to examine a small piece of skin, necessitated close proximity and inevitably involved physical contact.

'Mrs Ramsey has been coming to us for some years now,' Nick explained, when the first afternoon patient had fluttered into the room and kissed Nick far too heartily.

Phoebe told herself the pang she felt couldn't possibly be jealousy—one had to be involved with someone in order to be jealous and she certainly wasn't going to get involved with Nick! Nevertheless, she studied the woman who was chatting so familiarly to Nick.

Another blonde, but much older, perhaps a well-preserved fifty-something. Her hair, a burnished gold, swung lightly around an expertly made-up face. Her figure was slim and trim, a gym figure, exquisitely clothed in a mid-calf length skirt and matching blue-green shirt. Much the colour of Nick's eyes...

'Phoebe? Are you with us? This is your session, not mine.'

Phoebe ducked behind the screen where Mrs Ramsey was slipping out of the designer clothes. She handed the glamorous patient a gown then helped her up onto the examination table.

'We're onto legs at the moment,' the woman said to her, smiling conspiratorially. 'Either Nick or Charles have managed to remove most of the skin on my legs and arms already but they insist I keep on coming back. I think they're afraid they'll lose my husband's regular donations if they completely cure me.'

'Would that we could,' Nick said, arriving to stand beside Phoebe. 'I'd even give up Don's financial support.'

He bent over to examine the scarred tissue on their patient's legs.

'Fair-haired, blue-eyed, pale freckled skinned—a recipe for disaster as far as sun damage is concerned,' he muttered.

'Add a lifetime playing tennis in little short skirts and sleeveless tops—that didn't help,' Mrs Ramsey told Phoebe. 'Not to mention lying for hours on the beach in my teenage years, because of a craving to look tanned and fit, the golden Aussie archetype.'

'Most of the tumours we've removed have been SCCs,' Nick continued, 'squamous cell carcinomas, with a few basal cell carcinomas, the slow-growing but potentially malignant sun-damage lesions, as well, so I remove a narrow margin of skin around the edges of anything suspicious and test it for involvement.'

Phoebe knew he was explaining all this for the patient's sake, not hers, and, as she always did when working closely with him, admired the way in which he provided information so it was easy for the lay person to understand. Squamous cell carcinomas affected the top layer of the skin and usually began as solar keratosis with patches of raised or scaly skin. BCCs presented as small raised pink papules, which developed tiny craters in their centres.

She nodded as if the information was meant for her alone.

'I told you he'd practically skinned me,' Mrs Ramsey said.

Then Nick stepped back.

'OK, it's your turn, Dr Moreton. Have a look and tell me what you're going to do.'

Phoebe felt a spurt of unfamiliar panic fire through her body.

Why?

She'd taken clinics on her own dozens of times, and not panicked. Was it Nick's presence today, or the feeling that this might be some kind of test?

She put the unanswerable questions aside, put on her glasses, and bent to examine Mrs Ramsey's legs.

The scar tissue where lesions had been cut out or burnt off using liquid nitrogen was obvious, but there was another mark on the woman's left calf, embedded deep in old scarring.

Phoebe turned to the computer where the introductory page of Mrs Ramsey's file was on the screen.

'I just want to check something,' she said, although their patient was so deep in conversation with Nick, Phoebe doubted whether she'd heard.

She scrolled down until she came to images taken on the patient's previous visit. She enlarged the area she wanted to study and searched in vain for a pinkish spot like the one now visible on Mrs Ramsey's leg.

Turned back to the patient.

'I think there's a new problem here,' she said, indicating the site with her gloved finger.

Mrs Ramsey sighed, but Nick drew closer.

'OK, what will you do with it?' he asked.

Phoebe turned towards him. He was so close she could see pinpoints of gold in his blue-green eyes.

'I think it's a new BCC or perhaps a re-growth of an old one, but the skin is too thin to make another incision to remove it here and now. It's on the calf muscle and the slightest movement will aggravate the wound and complicate healing.'

'So?' he prompted.

She frowned, thinking through all she'd learned since she'd joined the team.

'Mohs' surgery? Excision of fine layers microscopically, under a light anaesthetic and a local nerve block. That way we can stain the tumour and only take extra tissue from around it if the malignancy has spread to cells beyond the wound. Then a skin graft, because the scar tissue would resist simple stitching.' She thought for a moment. 'But again, there could be problems with the graft taking on that part

of the leg. Hospitalisation, restricted movement, plastic skin to protect the graft?'

Nick straightened up and touched her lightly
on the shoulder.

'We might make a dermatologist of you
yet,' he said. The words caused even more
skittish reaction than the touch—if that was
possible.

When she'd been employed by the clinic, it
had been on the understanding that the position
wasn't connected to the specialist dermatology
programme. 'Because, as we don't do all the
general skin complaints, we're not considered
a teaching unit,' Nick had explained.

It hadn't bothered Phoebe at the time, as she
hadn't been certain she wanted to specialise.
In fact, she'd almost certainly decided not to
take on a specialty. But a general practitioner
with specialist knowledge in skin cancer could
do a lot of good in the course of his or her
normal work.

Now she wanted to query Nick about the
remark, but he was talking to Mrs Ramsey—
Elizabeth, he called her—explaining the surgery. The skin graft would use her own skin
which would be cut from a site probably on
her thigh, then, clever organ that it was, the

skin would replenish itself on both the donor site and on her leg.

He finished the examination Phoebe had begun while she watched the sure way his hands moved, noticed the slimness of his fingers, the fine dark hairs at the wrists, curling around the rolled edge of his gloves.

'Would you ask Sheree to fix some coffee and take it into my office?' he said to Phoebe as they left the patient to dress. 'I'll make the hospital arrangements for the surgery while Mrs Ramsey is here. I can leave you in charge?'

Phoebe nodded. Disappointment had risen like a tide in her throat, although that was stupid. So what if Nick had chosen to work the clinic because he'd known Mrs Ramsey had an appointment? It was none of Phoebe's business what he did!

She worked through the rest of the day, excising tiny tumours, curetting the simpler lesions by scraping the surface with a fine glass spoon-shaped instrument, then using an electric needle to seal the edges. When it came to problem tissue on patients where the cartilage might be damaged by other methods, she used cryotherapy.

'Noses and ears,' she said to Mr Bryant, as the spurt of liquid nitrogen froze the margin around the BCC on his ear lobe. 'They're nearly always exposed to the sunlight—on men, anyway. That's why those bits of the body are so vulnerable.'

But although she talked and joked with the patients, her mind still niggled away at Nick's behaviour. Or, more truthfully, at her reaction to Nick's behaviour.

At day's end, she went through to the small laboratory. Though short of a nurse, Ellen, their trusty lab assistant, had been on hand, setting, labelling and packaging the diseased tissue Phoebe had removed, dispatching one specimen from each lesion to Pathology for testing, leaving a second for the doctor's use.

Phoebe studied each in turn, making notes for herself which later she'd compare with the pathology reports. It was her way of testing herself, of checking that she was retaining the new knowledge she absorbed each day.

Nick guessed she'd be there, and although he had a mountain of paperwork to tackle in his office, and ward visits to make, he found his feet carrying him towards the lab. He paused in the doorway, studying the white-coated form bent over the microscope. Apart from the glossy dark hair, it could have been anyone, yet he felt if he'd been blindfolded he would still have known it was Phoebe.

The thought made him frown, and he had to remind himself of all the reasons why he didn't want to get involved with anyone at the moment. Particularly not an anyone like Phoebe Moreton. Though...

At that instant she must have sensed his presence for she glanced up, and he caught a glimpse of what looked like pleasure in her eyes before she blinked it away and asked, 'Do you want to do some work? Need the microscope? I'm just about done. I've been looking at today's slides.'

Did the rush of words indicate confusion? He rather hoped it did—it would make them a matched pair in that department.

Only his confusion, or so he told himself, was over whether or not to explain to Phoebe about Jess's past relationship with Charles. But whenever he considered the pain he'd see in Phoebe's dark eyes, he shied away from the idea.

'Well?' the object of his consternation demanded.

He felt his frown returning.

'I'm sorry. Thinking of something else. What did you say?'

She smiled at him, and he felt a sizzle of heat in his abdomen. It's pretend, he reminded himself. And she's not the kind of woman with whom you can play games. Added to which, she's already been hurt by one male in this department.

'I asked if you'd sorted out a date for Mrs Ramsey's op?'

Medical talk—that was better.

'Yes. I had to wangle theatre time and trade off some of our non-existent nurse's hours to staff it, but I'll operate next Monday. I'll do that lentigo maligna—Mr Webster—at the same time.' He sounded quite rational, and was congratulating himself on regaining control when he heard words he hadn't intended to say coming from his lips. 'Do you want to assist with Mrs Ramsey?'

Her face lit up as if he'd offered her a rare gift, so he could hardly take back the offer, but his physical reaction to that smile reminded him that sharing an operating microscope with Phoebe was going to put her body in very close proximity to his—not a good idea since the kiss.

Kisses—plural...

'I'd love to,' she assured him, stacking away the slides she'd been studying. 'I've never seen extensive Mohs' surgery performed.'

Well, *she* certainly wasn't worried by bodily proximity so he'd better get over it.

'How did Jessica's meeting with Mr Abrams go? Did you hear?'

The work-related question helped, and by the time he'd explained what Jess had suggested, using a digital camera to transfer images direct to a computer, he was more or less back in control.

'That's great,' Phoebe said, and she smiled again. Although he could have lived without the smile, he was intrigued by her obvious delight.

'Does it please you so much, to have a patient's fears lessened?'

She looked surprised, then nodded decisively.

'Of course it does,' she said stoutly. 'Isn't the practice of medicine all about reassurance?' She tossed her head so the weight of glossy hair shifted slightly, trapping light and throwing back gleams of red from its hidden depths.

'I know all the ''curing cancer'' trials and experiments attract more media attention—and consequently more money from government and donors—but most patients are interested in the here and now. They want whatever is wrong with them fixed or, if it can't be fixed, the pain of it alleviated. But more than anything else, they want reassurance.'

She spoke so seriously, Nick had to smile.

'Cures for cancer might be relevant to people when they're diagnosed with it,' he teased, but his smile wasn't reciprocated.

'I don't know about that!' she said, and once again the appearance of a tiny frown between her eyebrows made him want to smooth the crease away. 'I think people are becoming fairly cynical about the so-called miracle cures. Whenever something is hyped up on television, there are always white-coated scientists warning that it's only early days and clinical trials could be ten years away.'

'Clinical trials have begun on a vaccine for melanoma right here in this hospital,' he argued, letting himself be drawn into the conversation in the hope it might distract him from his too-personal thoughts.

'Vaccine!' Phoebe scoffed. 'When you use the word ''vaccine'' to the general public, they immediately assume they can go to their local doctor, ask for it and come out immune to melanoma for the rest of their natural lives.'

It was Nick's turn to frown.

'Do you really think that's what they expect when they see the publicity? I mean—'

'What's happening here is a very early trial,' she interrupted. 'And being conducted on patients who have advanced melanoma which has not been halted by conventional means. Yes, *I* know that, and *you* know that, but to most people, the word ''vaccine'' means something you're given to provide immunity. Generally for life.'

Immunity! Nick's mind skipped to a remark Phoebe had made—before the kiss. She was immune to men like him. Why? Or should the question be how?

A man in the past who'd betrayed her?

No! Surely she'd be more worldly, even cynical, if that were the case.

For a moment he wished she were. It was her apparent innocence that so attracted him, yet warned him at the same time to stay clear.

'But, in fact, all we're currently doing is altering cells and injecting them back into patients' bodies,' she continued, 'in the hope it might trigger the patients' own immune systems into fighting the tumours.'

He forgot Phoebe's immunity and innocence to take up the argument.

'But eventually, using this technology, if we detect defective genes which suggest a predisposition to melanoma, we can alter them to provide immunity.'

She stepped towards him, smiling again, and shuffled some notes she must have been making into a file.

'But who are you going to test? People with melanoma in their families, although only ten per cent of melanoma is familial?'

Nick shook his head.

'Boy, are you in an argumentative mood! Don't forget I was part of the research team involved in this project you're treating with such disdain. I know it's only a possible solution and success is a long way off as yet, but

every new development has to start somewhere.'

She chuckled, probably at his defensive
tone, and said, 'I know, and it makes me angry
that the work you did on the vaccine was then
taken over by the oncologists so now it's slot-
ted into the general cancer funding, rather than
the money coming to the clinic.'

Her voice belied her anger, at least for Nick,
who found it soothing. He watched her close
the folder and then hesitate, running her fingers
down the edge of the cardboard.

'They're welcome to the money if they can
find a cure,' he said, distancing himself from
thoughts of those fingers doing a similar tactile
exploration of his skin. 'All I'd like is enough
funding to perfect some foolproof system of
early diagnosis of the lesions which are likely
to be dangerous. A nodular melanoma can
arise very suddenly, then within weeks spread
into surrounding tissues. From there it's into
the blood and off to develop further tumours
in any organ of the body.'

'Patient education—and public awareness
campaigns. Surely that's where we have to
concentrate our efforts.' She shut the folder
into a drawer as she spoke, and looked directly

at him. 'But that just gets them to the doctor, doesn't it? Isn't that why the new computer program is so important?'

As the clear brown eyes looked into his, something else he should have told her niggled at his brain, but his body was overriding many of his mental processes, and he couldn't think of anything but kissing her again.

Phoebe heard the footsteps approaching and knew it was Charles. Looking for Nick, no doubt.

Anger stirred as she remembered the glares their colleague had been giving her, and the scathing remark he'd made earlier that day about her joining the ranks of 'Nick's women'. Well, she'd show him!

She smiled at Nick as she moved closer, murmured, 'It's all in a good cause,' then stood on tiptoe and kissed him on the lips.

He reacted as if stung, drawing back so suddenly she felt mortified. Then he must have remembered about the pretence, for he joined in, kissing her with the intensity she'd felt not yesterday in the cafeteria but that first afternoon in the corridor.

'Well, don't mind me!'

Charles's petulant tone penetrated the sensual haze enveloping Phoebe, and with diffi-
culty, she pushed away from Nick.

And summoned some cool!

'Did you want something, Charles?' she
asked, while covertly licking the taste of Nick
from her lower lip.

The silence which greeted her question
made her look directly at Charles—then at
Nick. Both men's attention seemed focussed
on her face—her mouth.

'I wondered if you were going home.'
Charles recovered first, though the words came
out slightly strangled. 'I lent my car to Jess—
she sold hers before she went away. I thought
I might hitch a ride with you.'

Out of the corner of her eye Phoebe saw
Nick, who'd stepped back towards the work-
bench, throw up his hands in an 'I give up'
kind of gesture, but Charles had driven her
home when she'd had transport problems, and
at least it was Jess, not Anne, he was helping
out this time.

Besides which, it might be a good thing.
Being close to Charles, even if it was only in
the physical confines of a car, might help her

regain the balance Nick's kisses were destroying.

Though the last one *had* been her fault...

'Sure, I'll drop you home,' she said, ignoring the eye rolling Nick was now doing. 'I'll
finish clearing up here, then get my things.
Fifteen minutes suit you?'

Charles nodded then walked away, and
Phoebe felt the tension wash from her body,
leaving her weak-kneed with relief.

Until Nick turned on her.

'What on earth are you doing?' he demanded. 'The moment he crooks his finger,
you go running! It's the "yes, Charles, no,
Charles" scenario all over again.'

'It *is* not!' Phoebe yelled her denial, then
realised she could hardly tell him she'd chosen
to drive Charles home in the hope it might re-
inforce the immunity she seemed to have lost.
She did a gathering-herself-together thing
again and said, 'I thought I handled it in a
totally mature fashion. I ignored his dig about
finding us kissing—'

'But licked your lip in case he'd missed it,'
Nick interjected.

The reminder caused a momentary glitch in
her composure, but she refused to be ruffled.

'I agreed to help him out,' she finished gamely. 'As a colleague, Nick David, nothing else.'

Nick caught back the growling 'It had better be nothing else' that had sprung to his lips. Whatever lay between himself and Phoebe was not real, he reminded himself. The very last thing he needed in his life was a complication like Dr Phoebe Moreton. She was too young, too innocent—wouldn't understand the dating-mating game he played when he needed a distraction.

Or why he played it, come to that!

She muttered something that might have been goodbye and swept from the room.

In high dudgeon, his mother would have said.

Which reminded him he should phone his mother. She'd be anxious for news of Peter, whom she'd welcomed as a fifth child the first time Nick had brought his mate home from boarding school.

And *that* train of thought reminded him of where his responsibilities lay for the next few months—maybe even years. With Peter Carter, patient and long-time best friend.

The diagnosis of Peter's melanoma while they'd still been at school had shocked them both, but while Peter had become resigned to it, Nick had never been able to accept that Peter's death from the disease was inevitable. That the death of any young person was inevitable! Since then, he'd been guided by a determination to do whatever he could to save—or at least prolong—his friend's life.

Not that squiring Phoebe to dinner and a ball would distract him too much from this goal— it was only one night, after all.

The mental argument made him sigh, and he sought diversion in work, crossing to the bench and finding the file Phoebe had put away. She'd been making her own notes on the sections she'd taken during the day. It was the kind of thing he'd done in his early days in dermatology, when he'd first entered the specialty programme.

'Oh, damn!' he muttered, belatedly remembering what it was he'd meant to tell her.

CHAPTER FIVE

CHARLES was waiting for Phoebe in the corridor. She expected more recriminations over her blatant exhibitionism with Nick, but Charles was subdued. Perhaps even distracted.

Don't start feeling sorry for him again, she warned herself, then studied him covertly as they walked out.

His blond good looks would have qualified him for male-model status, but why, when she'd first started working here, she'd found them more appealing than the dark, brooding beauty of Nick's features...

You recognised the playboy in Nick—all senses on instant alert, she reminded herself.

'...is looking for a new car, but it might take a while and as she lives out in the suburbs it seemed...'

Belatedly, Phoebe realised Charles had been talking—presumably about Jess and her transportation problems.

'But isn't it putting you out?' she asked. 'How are you supposed to get around?'

With great forbearance, she didn't add, 'and run after Anne?'

She glanced towards him as she asked the question and saw a faint wash of colour creep into his cheeks.

'She'll bring the car back this evening,' he said. 'Actually, there are a few private sales of vehicles that sound all right advertised in the local paper. I offered to help her check them out this evening. With both of us there, one can drive the second car if she decides to buy something.'

Phoebe felt a sense of *déjà vu*. This was exactly the kind of thing he'd done for Anne, often breaking an arrangement he'd already made with Phoebe to dance attendance on his ex-wife. Was he using Jess in retaliation to Phoebe's behaviour towards Nick?

She searched inside herself but could find no negative reaction to the thought.

Surely she should care?

It was Nick's fault. He'd caused such disorder in her senses she could no longer think straight, let alone react!

'You're playing with fire, you know.'

Once again, she had to haul herself out of deep introspection to focus on Charles's conversation.

'Driving you home?' she quipped, although she knew damn well what he meant. Hadn't she been telling herself much the same thing?

'Fooling around with Nick. You're not in his league, Phoebe. You don't understand the rules of the games men like Nick play.'

'I didn't understand the rules of the game you played, Charles,' she said bitterly, as every word he spoke punched into her like bullets, reinforcing what her common sense already knew but hurting nonetheless. 'You acted as if you liked me, as if I was special to you, but never took it further—always holding me at arm's length, putting me second to Anne.'

Her accusation ended the conversation. She unlocked the car and climbed in, waited until he'd adjusted his seat belt, then drove out of the car park.

Silence stretched between them, taut and uncomfortable.

I'll stop this nonsense with Nick, she decided, easing her way into a line of traffic held up at lights at an intersection ahead of them. Tell him I won't go to the ball.

'You might as well know I've asked Jess to accompany me to the ball. I assume you won't be accompanying me.'

First bullets, and now a slap in the face! Phoebe forgot all her good intentions.

'Of course I won't, I'm going with Nick,' she said brightly, then the devil inside her prompted her to get a little of her own back. 'Which reminds me, it's late night shopping tonight. Do you mind if I drop you at the bus stop? I saw a to-die-for dress in Rochelle's window and tonight might be the only chance I have to try it on. I'd be upset if I left it until the weekend and found it was sold.'

If the murderous expression on her companion's face was any guide, she'd scored!

'Drop me at the shopping centre, I'll get a cab,' he said, through lips so thinned the words barely filtered through.

'Great!' Phoebe enthused. 'I'm so sorry about this but I knew you'd understand.'

Charles didn't look particularly understanding.

Enraged might better describe his expression.

Perhaps she should have added 'After all, you've done it to me often enough' to make sure he got the point.

She swung off the road and into the huge parking area of the suburban shopping centre they both used. It wasn't far from here to Charles's townhouse, a few dollars in a cab, but guilt pricked regardless.

Until he got out when she stopped near the cab rank, then leaned back into the car to ask, 'Would you have needed this desperate dash to the shops if you'd been going to the ball with me?'

The door slammed shut before she could answer his taunt, and she had to relieve her anger with an unladylike oath only she could hear.

Once parked, she walked towards the low-set building, pondering the question he'd asked. He wasn't to know that she'd first seen the red dress when she'd been in the exclusive boutique, trying on the demure black one she'd bought to wear to the ball with Charles.

'Isn't it divine?' Rochelle had enthused, but Phoebe had imagined Charles's horrified reaction if she'd dared to wear such a shimmery, sexy, seductive slip of satin, and had shied away from it. However, it was exactly the kind of dress Nick's gorgeous blondes *would* wear. Which was, she realised now, why Charles's question had angered her! It was on a par with the 'joining the ranks of Nick's women' remark he'd made earlier!

But did she care?

No way!

Her pace increased, her feet rushing her towards the siren call of The Dress.

Heavens, but her life was taking on some capital letters. The Dress. The Kiss.

Heat simmered inside her at the memory. Memories!

'Concentrate on The Dress today,' she chided herself, then she smiled at the passer-by who'd caught her talking to herself.

'Wow!'

Rochelle's reaction to a red-satin-clad Phoebe didn't do much to alleviate the doubts she herself was having.

'It's very low,' she told Rochelle, peering dubiously down at the expanse of white breast showing in the cleavage.

'Only from your perspective because you're looking straight down,' Rochelle reminded her. 'Stop trying to tug it higher and look at yourself in the mirror. That's how other people will see you.'

Phoebe steeled herself for another glance at her reflection.

Nothing had changed since she'd last looked. There, opposite her, was a stranger— a sultry, sexy, curvy stranger in a dress that shrieked seduction.

'I—I couldn't wear it,' she stuttered, as embarrassment for the person in the mirror made her blush. 'It probably looks gorgeous on someone slim but it's practically indecent on me.'

'Nonsense!' Rochelle told her. 'It's made for someone like you. Skinny women don't do anything for dresses like this, In fact, I wouldn't sell it to someone less, well, less well-endowed, shall we say?'

The scorching heat in Phoebe's cheeks told her, without looking, that her blush had deepened. Any minute now she'd be as red as the dress.

'Special occasion?' Rochelle asked, twitching at the skirt where a slit revealed a brave length of white thigh.

Was it?

'Yes!' Phoebe heard herself saying, so much challenge in her voice she barely recognised it.

'Well, that's just the dress you want for it!' Rochelle assured her. 'You'll knock him dead, whoever he is.'

The words should have provided assurance, but instead confused Phoebe even more. It was to show Charles that she coveted the dress, wasn't it?

But the man dropping dead with delighted surprise in her mental image wasn't Charles. And perhaps fainting would be a better analogy than dropping dead...

She studied her image more dispassionately this time and accepted, finally, that buying this dress had nothing to do with Charles, and a whole lot to do with Nick.

Though the danger implicit in playing games with Nick made her shiver at her own temerity.

'I'll take it,' she said, turning resolutely away from the mirror in case she weakened.

'You'll need shoes,' Rochelle reminded her, helping Phoebe with the zip. 'I saw a divine pair of vivid red sandals with high spike heels in that little shoe shop next to the deli.'

Phoebe took a deep breath. The dress was going to put pressure on her credit card. Add shoes, and her budget for the next three months would be blown. Did she really want to do this?

Especially when instinct suggested the monetary price she'd pay for the dress and spike-heeled shoes might turn out to be the least of her worries.

'I'll wrap it?' Rochelle said, when Phoebe slipped the dress out through the door of the changing room.

Another deep breath—and an anticipatory thrill as she imagined Nick's reaction to this very different Phoebe.

'Yes,' she said firmly, 'and thanks for the tip about the sandals. I'll go straight there to try them on.'

She drove home eyeing the parcels on the passenger seat and wondering if she'd lost her mind. First dumping Charles out of the car when she'd already agreed to drive him home, and then, on a whim, buying not only a red dress but exotic red sandals as well.

Sexy red sandals.

The kind of footwear Mindy would wear.

The thought of her father's latest wife reminded her that she'd meant to visit him this evening, but by now they'd probably gone out to dinner. As far as she could remember, none of his wives—after her mother who'd been number one in timing but not importance—had ever been able to cook. Coupled with his dislike of having staff living in his house, it made dining out every night a necessity.

Anyway, now she'd bought the dress, she'd have to keep up the game with Nick at least until the ball. Which meant it wasn't quite so urgent to visit her father for a booster shot against men like him—and like Nick—who, for all their charm and flirty eyes, had an aura of primal danger about them.

She'd see her father next week.

Friday was day-surgery day. Phoebe, feeling bad about her behaviour towards Charles and determined not to let Nick tease him in the car park, arrived early.

She unlocked the outer door and walked into their suite of rooms, flicking on lights as she went. There was a pile of paper on Sheree's desk, Nick's distinctive scrawl across them suggesting he'd worked late last night. Phoebe crossed to the desk at the back of the office which had been designated hers when she'd come to work in the unit.

'The place was only set up for two doctors and it's taken me years to get the funding for an extra pair of trained hands,' Nick had explained apologetically when he'd pointed out she wouldn't have an office.

A single sheet of paper, centred neatly on her desk, was covered with the same writing.

Phoebe dropped her handbag into the bottom filing drawer, all the while peering at the note. Not yet willing to read it, although that was stupid. Nick often left her work-related notes, and this was hardly likely to be anything else.

In the end, she reached out and picked it up, telling herself she couldn't possibly be suffering palpitations over a letter from her boss.

'Phoebe,' it began. 'Charles is taking the day surgery today. Admin has promised a nurse, so could you do the morning ward round of our hospitalised patients then sit in on the specialists' discussion? The visitors from the US will be there, and Malcolm wants someone from our unit to show the flag.'

Phoebe glanced at the clock. Morning ward rounds began promptly at eight-thirty, but she had plenty of time. She booted up her computer and when the antiquated machine had decided it was ready for work she searched for the files of hospitalised patients.

Although she regularly visited the clinic's patients when they were undergoing chemotherapy as inpatients at the hospital, she needed to know exactly where they were up to in their treatment before joining the major ward round of the week.

Sheree came in as she was sighing over Jackie Stubbings. Jackie had only been sixteen when the deadly cells from an undetected melanoma had spread through her body. Now, after extensive treatment and nearly three years in remission, she was back in hospital, with new tumours in her left lung and brain.

'How's she doing?' Sheree asked, seeing the teenager's file on Phoebe's screen.

'Radiation has reduced the size of the tumours. I guess the specialists will have new scans to show today. After that they'll have to decide whether to operate on one or both tumours, when and how, then how much chemo and radiotherapy she's going to need.'

'Poor kid!' Sheree said. 'It's cases like hers make me wish I worked somewhere else. I know we get all excited about the patients where we do find trouble in time to stop it spreading, but knowing once it's gone as far as it has with Jackie it's practically hopeless... It makes me want to get out!'

'I know,' Phoebe agreed. 'But we're saving far more than we're losing. Look at it from that angle.'

Sheree shot her a sardonic look.

'You're a veritable ray of sunshine today. Coming to your senses about Charles has obviously done you some good.'

Phoebe wasn't surprised to hear that Sheree knew of the situation between herself and Charles, but the 'coming to your senses' phrase puzzled her. She was about to ask what Sheree had meant when Charles walked in and the moment was lost.

'I thought you were doing the ward round,' he said to Phoebe, speaking coldly into the air somewhere above her head.

'I'm on my way,' she said, and ducked past him, more anxious to escape him than to hear an explanation of Sheree's remark.

'So they're finally letting you out of that shoe-box down there.' Malcolm Graham, the senior oncologist at Southern Cross, greeted Phoebe with a smile. 'You know Geoff Kerr and Fran Neibling?'

Phoebe nodded and smiled at the two doctors who worked on the oncology ward. She'd met them the first time she'd visited melanoma patients and now saw them often on her regular visits to the ward.

'We've talked to Mrs Stubbings and Jackie, and surgeons will operate on the lung later this week,' Malcolm explained to Phoebe. 'She'll continue radiation on the brain tumour, and start chemo for the lung as soon as she's well enough.'

'What's shown up on the latest scan?' Phoebe asked, as Malcolm showed no sign of beginning the round. Probably waiting for the visitors.

'Nothing new as yet,' Fran told her, but her tone of voice confirmed Phoebe's own fears. New tumours could be growing anywhere in Jackie's body.

'After her, we'll visit Mrs Warren and then Peter Carter last of all,' Malcolm said, covering the three melanoma patients currently receiving treatment in the hospital.

Phoebe felt a jolt of excitement in her chest. Peter Carter was their test case, a scientist who'd agreed to try the radical new 'vaccine'. Other hospitals in other places were working on similar projects, but Peter was their first and if he continued to improve then it was possible, if conventional methods of treatment failed for Jackie, she, too, could be treated in this way.

Two men in beautifully cut suits approached.

'Ha! Our guests,' Malcolm murmured, stepping forward to shake hands with both men.

'Bill Cotter and Professor Brad Moss,' Malcolm said, then introduced his staff.

It made them a big bunch to be moving from room to room in the hospital, so Phoebe hung back, there to answer questions if required but otherwise trying to keep out of the way.

'So, you're a specialist dermatologist?' Bill said, when they'd gathered in the doctors' room for a post-round discussion, and he'd settled into a chair next to hers.

'Not yet, she's not,' Malcolm replied for her. 'But she's representing our skin cancer unit this morning. You met Nick David, who heads the unit, when he was over in the States. He'll join us for lunch and you'll see him again this evening.'

The conversation moved on to the new treatment, and Peter Carter's progress, but Phoebe, although she was glad to hear of the continuing decrease in tumour size since Peter had been vaccinated with cells developed from his own tumour, only half listened. Puzzling instead over Malcolm's first remark.

Not yet she's not!

It was the second time in as many days that someone had mentioned the possibility—or even probability—of her specialising. A decision she had not yet made, and probably never would make. Not when GP work still seemed to her to promise more long-term fulfilment.

By lunchtime Phoebe was back in the unit. A murmur of voices from Nick's office suggested he was in, but had company and, as the reception area was empty Phoebe assumed it was Sheree in with him.

So she was surprised when the door opened and Jess came out.

She greeted Phoebe with delight.

'Are you busy or would you like to have lunch with me?' she asked. 'Nick's turned me down. Says he has more important fish to fry. You're not needed until the afternoon skin clinic, are you?'

Phoebe found herself saying, no, she wasn't needed until later, and, yes, she'd go to lunch, though with a reluctance it was hard to define. Much as she knew she *should* tell Jess why Nick was showing an interest in her, the reluctance had spread to that as well.

She followed Jess as they wove their way through staff and visitors towards the canteen, admiring the woman's slim back, her blonde hair, her air of utter confidence.

Definitely a Nick-type woman!

So when they'd finally settled at a table, healthy lunches in front of them, and Jess said, 'I suppose either Nick or Sheree have told you about my abortive love affair with Charles,' Phoebe nearly fell off her chair.

'Your what with who?' she demanded.

'Whom,' Jess corrected gently, a small, self-mocking smile playing around her lips. 'Charles, that's with whom! Stupid wasn't it, to fall in love with a man who's still so obsessed with his ex-wife?'

She sighed and gazed off into the space, which gave Phoebe time to collect her scattered wits.

Scattered wits, and misbehaving body parts—she was coming to pieces both mentally and physically.

Think about Charles, not trivia. About Jess and Charles.

At least she hadn't been the only one who'd mistaken sympathy for something stronger!

But was that relevant?

Of course not.

'You're not saying much,' Jess said, and Phoebe tried to rein in the random thoughts—to find an appropriate response.

'You and Charles?' she muttered, which wasn't as appropriate as it might have been. 'No,' she added lamely. 'No one had told me!'

Which diverted her thoughts even further. No one—namely Nick—had told her. He must have known, the moment Jess had come back, that the pretence—the making-Charles-jealous act—was unnecessary.

New anger built! Just wait, Nick David. Just you wait!

'And I really thought I was over him and it was safe to come back but, seeing him again, and seeing how unhappy Anne still makes him, it's just as bad as ever.'

Phoebe concentrated on what Jess was saying. She'd deal with Nick later. Jess was smiling wanly at her, inviting comment or advice.

'Do you love him?' Phoebe asked the obvious question, and Jess's smile faded.

'Yes, I do. Stupid, isn't it?'

Join the club as far as stupidity is concerned, Phoebe thought bitterly, although fortunately, now she consider it, she'd never quite got to loving him. She'd been more in love with the idea of Charles, with his seriousness and apparent stability. With his resemblance to her youthful image of the ideal man!

To Jess she said, 'Then you have to do something about it. Have you considered talking to Anne? Finding out if there's any hope of the pair of them getting back together? I mean, if she actually wants him back, there's probably no future for you, but if she tells you there's no way, then all you have to do is convince Charles it's over and you're the one for him.'

Her inner self laughed hollowly as she recited things she'd considered doing herself. At

least she hadn't suggested Jess try to make
Charles jealous!

An image of the physical violence she'd like
to inflict on Nick David rose in the wake of
that thought. He'd encouraged her to believe
she could make Charles jealous, and used that
excuse to kiss her into total confusion.

Why?

For laughs?

'I suppose I could do that,' Jess was saying
dubiously, and Phoebe had to rein in her tu-
multuous thoughts and concentrate on here and
now. 'What do you think about trying to make
him jealous? If Nick's free, and you said
there's nothing going on between you, perhaps
he'd be willing to pretend to be interested in
me!'

A scrunch of something that couldn't possibly be jealousy tightened Phoebe's stomach
muscles.

'What a good idea,' she said lamely. 'But
what would Nick's current girlfriend, whoever
she might be, think of it?'

To Phoebe's surprise, Jess laughed.

Heartily!

'Nick's current girlfriend?' She chortled.
'Don't tell me you've been fooled by his

harem of lovely blondes? Window-dressing, that's what he calls them. He reckons a gorgeous woman on his arm improves the donations he receives by several thousand dollars a time. I've even stood in on occasion, when none of the women he knows were available.'

Phoebe absorbed this information with mixed emotions. There was relief in there, but the anger which had been growing since Jess's confession still simmered, and the idea of Nick using women in such a way turned up the heat.

Unfortunately, it also aroused her curiosity.

'But if they're just window dressing what about his love life? Are you saying a man like Nick doesn't have one?'

Jess grinned at her.

'Unbelievable, isn't it? Not that he's my type—unfortunately—but it's true. He claims he hasn't the time to give to a long-term relationship but I sometimes wonder if it's just that he hasn't met the right woman. As for sex, I've no idea what kind of arrangement he has with the women he dates, whether there's sex involved or not. There probably is, with a man like Nick, but I *do* know he believes it's not fair to any woman to get too involved while he's so focussed on work.'

Phoebe absorbed this blunt appraisal of Nick's love life with astonishment. She'd been so busy herself, getting through her studies, that she had to go back to her teenage years to remember discussing anyone's sex life, presumed or otherwise.

Fortunately, Jess had turned the conversation back to Charles and was happily describing how close and intimate they'd been, in between his forays to rescue Anne from some dilemma. Heat of a different kind rose to Phoebe's cheeks and, as she hoped her embarrassment wasn't too noticeable, she realised why she hadn't been part of these conversations for so long.

She'd had nothing to contribute!

Not a thing!

Once she'd got past a few teenage fumbles in the cramped confines of small student cars, her practical experience of sex had been nil, though medical studies had given her a wealth of theoretical knowledge.

While as far as Charles was concerned, a goodnight kiss on the cheek, or an occasional peck on the lips, was as far as *her* relationship had progressed.

She pasted an expression she hoped looked knowledgable on her face, and behind this mask gave serious thought to her virginity. No doubt it had arisen, originally, from hang-ups over her father's behaviour but, until today, it had never bothered her. Now Jess was speaking to her, woman to woman, expecting Phoebe to understand what she was saying— to answer questions about sexual intimacy she'd never experienced.

A couple of bland, meaningless phrases seemed to suffice, for Jess kept talking, extolling Charles's expertise as a lover. It caused a momentary pang in the region of Phoebe's heart to realise Charles had never cared enough for her to go beyond those few sedate kisses.

Or had he guessed at her inexperience and decided she wasn't a good candidate for sex?

'Though I reckon Nick would know a trick or two,' Jess was saying, when Phoebe tuned in again. 'Not that I'd ever be unfaithful to Charles, if he ever gets rid of Anne, but I think we women are entitled to a little experimentation, don't you?'

All Phoebe could manage this time was a strangled sound, then, gathering herself together yet again, she muttered something about being late for the clinic and dashed from the room.

But Jess's words remained with her, and alongside the anger she felt towards Nick for not telling her of Jess's and Charles's relationship was the early bud of an idea—a plan!

With a capital P?

Given her physical reactions to Nick's kisses, and Jess's opinion of his prowess in that field, wouldn't he make the perfect partner for her sexual initiation?

What's more, she'd be striking a blow for womankind. She would use him the way he apparently used women—as playthings to be discarded.

It could also have the added benefit of getting him right out of her system. Rebuild the immunity she seemed to be losing.

'So, who's doing what and with whom this afternoon?' Nick asked as she walked into her shared office to find both him and Charles with the secretary.

Fiery heat surged into Phoebe's cheeks as the words took on a meaning Nick would never guess at. She wondered just how red she'd gone. Especially when Sheree said,

'You're looking flushed. Are you feeling all right?'

'I hurried back from lunch,' she said, but the speculative gleam in Nick's eyes suggested he was replaying his question in his mind. She forgot The Plan and reminded herself she was angry with him. Though why he'd suggested the jealousy charade kept niggling in her mind...

'I've a pile of reports to get out to referring doctors,' Charles said. 'Then Jess is coming in to see if she can upgrade the density detecting capabilities of the computer program.'

He looked at Nick, ignoring Phoebe.

'So if you or Phoebe can take the clinic...'

Nick glanced towards their junior colleague. Something was going on in that pretty head. Had she guessed the truth about Charles and Jess? And, if so, was she upset about it?

'Charles will be here as back-up, so will you take it, Phoebe?' he asked. 'It's all regulars coming in for check-ups. There might be a few lesions to be burnt off, but there shouldn't be anything major.'

She nodded, but it was a distracted movement, doing little more than shift the thick dark tresses momentarily. There was certainly something bothering her.

Perhaps he should get over his stupid reluctance to tell her about Charles's previous relationship.

'Is no one going to ask where I'll be?' he said, bringing his mind firmly back to work-related matters.

Sheree chuckled.

'As if we need to ask,' she teased him. 'Peter's getting his next lot of treated cells. If you're far from his bedside for the next few days, we'll all be very surprised.'

'Well, prepare to be surprised,' he retorted. 'Phoebe and I have a date tonight, don't we, sweetheart?'

He turned towards Phoebe as he added the endearment and was surprised by her reaction. If looks could have killed, he'd be lying dead on the floor.

Was it the 'sweetheart' that had upset her?

But surely that was how he was supposed to be behaving?

Had she forgotten the making-Charles-jealous idea?

Which, of course, was the only reason he'd used it.

Wasn't it?

He made a general farewell noise and left the room, furious with himself for getting embroiled in such a foolish enterprise, particularly within a work unit as small as theirs.

Yet, as he walked through the hospital to the lab where Peter's tumour cells had been cultured, he realised he didn't want to pull out of the scheme—didn't want to not have an excuse to see more of Phoebe, if that made sense.

Not a lot of sense, the logical part of his mind responded. But, then, nothing much did these days.

Phoebe worked through the afternoon, patient after patient arriving to have superficial lesions checked or burnt off their legs, faces, chests, backs or arms.

'Ouch! That really stings,' an older man who'd spent a lifetime working outdoors in a singlet and shorts complained when Phoebe targeted a keratosis on the back of his upper arm.

'It's a touchy spot,' she agreed, dabbing more of the numbing local anaesthetic over the next lesion before she attacked it with the liquid nitrogen. 'You know the procedure when you get home. Dab them with methylated spirits to dry them out. Keep them uncovered in-doors but covered outdoors.'

She reeled off the usual warnings and pre-cautions, information most long-term patients knew by heart, but her mind kept straying to the idea she'd had—The Plan—weighing up the pros and cons, telling herself it was stupid, while enjoying the small tremors of excitement even thinking about it caused. Though it had to be attraction, not love, causing the tremors, and surely sleeping with Nick would cure her of that.

CHAPTER SIX

PHOEBE opened the door to Nick on the stroke of seven-thirty. Clad in his version of 'good casual'—pale chinos and a dark tan sweater that moulded itself to the heavy muscles of his chest—he was enough to make any woman's heart race. Any woman this side of dead, anyway.

Phoebe forgot how angry she was with him. Forgot she'd intended demanding to know why he'd suggested the jealousy charade. She also blotted all thought of The Plan from her mind, and made a valiant effort to act naturally.

She waved him into the living room.

'So, how's Peter?' she asked, thinking work would be a good topic while she got over whatever was making her breathless.

The smile on Nick's face faded, and she noticed a greyness in his skin and something like despair in his blue eyes.

'As well as can be expected, I guess.' He thrust his fingers through his hair, shook his head and muttered an oath under his breath. 'I loathe those trite doctor statements, and here I am making them myself.'

He tried a smile, but it was a wan effort.

'Sorry! I'd decided to put it out of my mind for the evening and at least pretend to be having a good time. Now I've put a dampener on it for you. As if you didn't have enough of that with Charles!'

Phoebe grabbed his arm and hustled him towards a chair.

'Sit!' she ordered, pointing to her comfortable leather recliner. 'I'll pour you a drink. Why on earth did you agree to go out tonight when you'd rather be with Peter? And don't you dare blame me. You'd already made the arrangements to wine and dine the visitors before I entered the picture.'

She crossed to the small bar in the corner of the room and found the aged Glenlivit whisky her father had provided for the regular occasions when he called in to have a sociable drink with her.

Pouring a small measure into a glass, she added ice and a few drops of water, then walked back to where Nick was now reclining, eyes closed, in her favourite chair.

'Here! I know you drink whisky. It's not enough to put you over the limit, but if you want another one when you've finished that, I'll drive you wherever you want to go. Although if it's back to the hospital you'd better stick to one.'

He opened one eye and squinted up at her.

'Just when did you get so bossy?'

She shrugged but didn't answer, too busy thinking how at home he looked, in *her* chair, in *her* living room.

The eye had closed and he sipped at the drink, then she saw his chest rise and fall as he heaved a huge sigh.

'That's beautiful, and your offer sounds like heaven, but I—we—really should do the dinner thing tonight, sweet Phoebe.'

He sat up straight, adjusting the chair to an upright position. Opened his eyes and looked at her as if seeing her for the first time.

'Particularly as you're looking so ravishing, young lady. I can't have you all dressed up with nowhere to go.'

The compliment caused more of the tremors she'd been suffering, although she'd have argued the 'young lady' bit if he hadn't been so obviously stressed.

'I could always go back to the hospital with you,' she suggested. 'That's if Peter wouldn't mind having two visitors instead of one.'

She saw Nick's eyes darken, as if his thoughts were displeasing, but when he put down his drink and beckoned to her, the words he spoke were gruff but not cross.

'Come here.'

She went, stopping by the side of the chair, shifting the drink a millimetre on the coaster.

His hand closed around her wrist and he tugged at her, surprise and tactics combining to land her in his lap where he held her captive with his arms around her waist.

'You are too nice for your own good,' he said sternly, the words a warm breath against her neck. 'No wonder Charles took advantage of you.'

'Charles never took advantage of me!' Phoebe told him, hoping a bit of indignation might halt the escalating excitement she was feeling.

Nick chuckled then qualified the statement.

'Of your good nature, I meant, although you sound slightly regretful about the other inter-pretation of that phrase.'

He pulled her closer and dropped a kiss on the top of her shoulder where her silk T-shirt must have slipped a little to expose some skin.

'I thought we were talking about Peter. About visiting the hospital,' Phoebe managed, though her nerves were on fire and her brain back in crash mode, while excitement skittered like marauding ants beneath her skin.

She felt him sigh again.

'I guess we were, though I'd far rather be talking about you. About what makes Phoebe tick and whether, beneath that serene exterior, there's hidden fire and passion.'

He pressed another kiss against the same patch of bare skin, and the ants went berserk.

'Definitely fire and passion if those kisses are any indication,' he murmured, while flames ignited in her blood and she wondered if he could feel her shaking.

'N-nonsense,' she managed to stutter. 'What you see is what you get!'

She took the opportunity of a slight slackening in his grip to remove herself from the tempting perch.

'Peter?' she reminded him.

'Yes, Peter!' he murmured, the words little louder than a sigh.

He picked up the drink and drained the remnants of it, then stood up.

'I *will* go back to the hospital. But first we'd better do our duty and dine with our visitors from overseas.'

'Nonsense!' Phoebe told him, her heart aching for him as he fought to put duty before his desire to be with his friend. 'You're far too concerned about Peter to be bothered making polite conversation. It's not as if they won't have hospital representatives with them at dinner. Charles will be there, and Malcolm Graham.'

She remembered Malcolm Graham's ambiguous remark and was about to ask Nick about it when she realised he was smiling at her in a way that made her toes tingle nearly as badly as the kiss had.

'I've never seen this ''mother hen'' side of you before. I can see why poor Charles ended up so muddled. It could become very addictive.' A glint of laughter twinkled in his eyes. 'So what do you suggest we do? Phone the restaurant and plead an emergency? No, that's no good. You miss out as well. Why don't you go to dinner and I'll go to the hospital?'

Phoebe felt a knife-thrust of disappointment so sharp she almost gasped.

'Considering the only reason you asked me to go was so Charles would see us together, that's a stupid suggestion.' She scowled crossly at him. 'If you don't want me at the hospital, that's fine. I'm not going to be broken-hearted over missing one dinner date. Especially as it was a put-up job anyway!'

He stepped towards her, then stepped back again, and had it been anyone but Nick she'd have read indecision into the movement. As it *was* Nick, she assumed his concern for the patient was overriding everything else.

'I think Peter would be delighted to see you at the hospital,' he said, then he smiled again and added, 'Any male this side of dead would be delighted.'

His use of the expression she'd thought but hadn't said made Phoebe study him more closely. No hint of the smile had reached his eyes this time. In fact, if anything, they looked bleak and desolated.

She took his arm. So what if he thought her a mother hen.

'Let's go, then,' she said. 'If I drive, you can phone the restaurant on the way and make our excuses.'

'No, I'll drive and you can make the phone call,' he said, and Phoebe grinned to herself. That was more like the Nick she knew! Taking charge—giving orders—organising!

It was after eight when they arrived on the ward and most visitors had already left. Peter was in a single room, lying with his head turned towards the wall.

'How's it going, mate?' Nick asked, as they walked quietly in.

The still-young man turned towards him and Phoebe saw his painfully thin shoulders lift in a shrug.

'I feel so frustrated!' he muttered. 'I know you keep telling me I probably need more doses, but the damn disease is travelling faster than our engineered cells can conquer it. When I've had the treatment, like today, it's as if I can feel those cells racing through my blood, but I can also feel the malignant tissues multiplying and I know which ones are going to win.'

He paused, then hitched himself up in the bed so he could look Nick in the eye.

'I can't help feeling that if I die, you'll see the trial as a failure and won't try it on Jackie, but I know somewhere down the track it's going to work. Maybe she'll be the success story, Nick.'

Phoebe swallowed hard as the import of Peter's concerns struck her.

'We've already applied for permission to try the protocols on Jackie,' Nick assured their patient. 'And we know the vaccine has decreased the size of some of your tumours. It's going to work for a lot of people, Peter, and, yes, Jackie could well be one of them.'

'Promise me that!' Peter demanded. 'Promise me one failure won't stop the trials.'

'Of course it won't,' Nick promised him. 'Phoebe can be my witness. Though why you're talking about such things when I've brought a gorgeous brunette to visit you, I don't know.'

Peter straightened up in bed and smiled apologetically at Phoebe.

'Trust you to get the priorities right, mate!' he said to Nick.

'I think you've got *your* priorities right,' she told Peter. 'Why shouldn't you be concerned about your health?'

Peter nodded his head towards Nick.

'This guy will tell you I should leave it to him. He's been telling me that since we were fifteen.'

Phoebe looked from Peter to Nick and repeated the words as a question.

'Since you were fifteen? I knew you were friendly but hadn't realised it was more than a doctor-patient thing. No one told me.'

'Not so much friends as thrown together at an early age—twelve, in fact—and forced to put up with each other,' Peter said, but a fondness in his voice belied the casual statement. 'We both ended up in the same boarding school. I'd lost my parents in a boating accident and Nick's mother felt he needed some masculine influence in his life.'

Nick backed up the statement but Phoebe barely listened. Though shocked by the revelation that Peter was an orphan, she couldn't help wondering how she'd feel if someone close to her was battling for his or her life. Being a doctor would make it worse, she decided. Add a sense of futility. No wonder Nick was under such a strain.

The urge to touch him, to take his hand, hold him in his arms as if her body could offer comfort, was so strong it shocked her and she moved to the other side of the bed to put herself out of harm's way.

And thought about this revelation.

'Obviously on another planet.' Nick's words intruded into her muddled mind.

'Or so bored by your company she's tuned out,' Peter teased. 'I don't blame her. Fancy bringing a doctor to a hospital on a date.'

'It's not a date,' she mumbled when she realised she was the subject of their conversation. 'Not a real date and, anyway, I suggested it.'

'Only because he was doing his hang-dog look, I bet. He'd get away with murder if the cop was a woman and he tried it on her.'

Nick started to argue, but Peter lifted his hand to stop him.

'Get out of here!' he ordered. 'You've already made a career of me, but I don't want you mooning over me every time I get new treatment. Take Phoebe somewhere nice—and I don't count going out to dinner with those visiting Americans as nice, so you can jolly well do better than that! Off you go!'

He waved his hand as if to shoo them from his room.

Nick studied his friend's face and guessed he was tireder than he was willing to admit.

'OK, I can take the hint,' he said. 'Not that you fool me for an instant with this concern for Phoebe. You've got that sexy red-headed nurse coming on duty and you want us out of here.'

He leaned forward to touch Peter lightly on the shoulder.

'See you, mate!'

He glanced towards Phoebe who was standing uncertainly by the bed.

'Come on, we're out of here. Patient's orders!'

She smiled, but at Peter not him.

'Take care,' she said softly, then she, too, touched their patient lightly on the shoulder— her fingers lingering against his skin.

'Heed your own warning, young lady,' Peter told her, waggling his head towards Nick as if to warn her of danger.

Her smile widened, something mischievous coming into it.

'Oh, I will,' she promised Peter, then she walked out the door, some mechanical combination of high heels and a tight skirt making her rear view so seductive Nick felt his groin tighten with desire.

'She's too innocent for your games,' Peter warned him, and Nick groaned.

'Don't I know it, Pete!' he said. 'And you're no help. Practically pushing us out the door.'

Peter ignored this accusation, merely eyeing Nick speculatively for a moment before saying, 'Have you told your mum you're seeing her?'

The change in subject startled Nick.

'Of course not! Actually, I'm not seeing her at all. She's using me to make Charles jealous.'

'And I'm going to walk out of here a cured man tomorrow!' Peter retorted. 'Get out of here. Go!'

Nick went, but although his legs moved, his mind was stuck, bogged in uncertainty.

'What did Peter mean about telling your mother about me?' Phoebe demanded, as they walked the maze of corridors leading out of the hospital.

'Peter talks too much!' Nick growled, hoping his 'date' would let the subject drop. He was having enough trouble thinking straight, especially now the perfume she was wearing had infiltrated his senses and was adding to the addled state of his brain.

But the hope was doomed to disappointment, he realised, when Phoebe pressed closer to avoid a group of nurses heading on duty and said, 'Surely you don't tell your mother about *all* your women!'

'You make me sound like Casanova, or some Arab sheik with a harem,' he grumbled, while the effect of soft breasts pressed against his arm added to the tightness in his lower abdomen. 'But if you must know, yes, I do tell my mother about *all* my women! Like most women, she's a master strategist and this is a defensive ploy I've developed.'

Phoebe stiffened and drew away from him, probably upset over his generalisation of her species. At least it put a little space between them. Heaven forbid she should detect his reaction!

'Defensive ploy indeed!' She iced the words with scorn. 'Sounds more like boasting to me.'

Nick sighed. His brain was numb, his body was misbehaving and the only thing he knew for certain was that he didn't want to be having this conversation with Phoebe Moreton.

'Where would you like to eat?' he asked, and silently congratulated himself on such a successful change in topic. A woman who enjoyed her food as much as Phoebe did would obviously have to give the question serious consideration.

'Oh, I don't mind,' she said, shooting that theory out of the sky. 'I'm not particularly hungry.'

She sounded slightly puzzled by this phenomenon—as well she might.

'Perhaps you're sickening for something.'

The suggestion was greeted with a wry smile.

'Now, there's a dreadful thought,' she said. 'It takes a mighty strong bug to put me off my tucker.'

She spoke lightly, but Nick thought he could detect concern in the dark liquid depths of her eyes.

Though she looked healthy enough.

Radiantly so.

Dangerously so!

Then, in full awareness of all the implications, he heard himself saying, 'My unit is only a few minutes' drive from here. I've a gem of a cleaning lady who stocks up my refrigerator every Friday. Would you like to check out what's available in the way of a snack?'

Phoebe felt a quiver of alarm race along her nerves, and warning signals, as loud and insistent as an ambulance siren, sounded in her head. Then she remembered how lost she'd felt during Jess's lunchtime conversation, and the seed of an idea it had planted.

The Plan!

'Sounds good to me,' she said, imbuing the words with just the right amount of casual, although her heart was beating wildly and her intestines knotting in such a way eating would be impossible.

Nick took her arm, which made things worse, and steered her through the wide foyer and out into the night air.

The shiver was involuntary, a reaction to her decision to pursue this foolish whim.

'Cold?' Nick murmured, picking up on the shiver and putting his arm around her so she could draw warmth from his body.

'N-not really,' she managed to stutter, while her brain told her the whole idea of getting Nick to help rid her of the burden of virginity was ridiculous. And the likelihood of his doing anything tonight was as far off as the moon.

Her upward glance was involuntary, so she was quite surprised to find there *was* a moon tonight—already riding high and gleaming silvery golden in the sky—shedding moondust with blithe disregard for the consequences.

'Full moon,' she heard Nick murmur, then his head blocked out the pale orb and his lips met hers, tasting rather than claiming, then going beyond claim to demand.

She gave in. Without the slightest hesitation or show of uncertainty, caught by the insidious magic his lips could weave, answering the demands with questions of her own. Kissing him back as desperately as if her life depended on it.

Warmth curdled in her blood, making thought impossible. It pooled in her abdomen and set up an ache in her thighs. She felt his hands on her shoulders, around her waist, one moving to her breast. She pressed closer, drawing heat and excitement in equal measure from his touch, his body.

Her fingers, skimming up his neck, drove softly into his hair, the silky feel of it sending ripples of sensation along her nerves. As the kiss deepened, she pressed closer to his body, clinging to him as if afraid to let go lest she be lost in the wondrous depths of sensations she didn't understand.

He moved away first, lifting his head and leaving her lips cold and lonely, releasing his grip on her so suddenly her legs had trouble taking over her support. She removed her hands more slowly, wanting to cry out with disappointment—and possibly frustration, if that's what the other feeling was. But it was important that he shouldn't guess at her reaction so she rallied—forced her mind to work.

'Pity Charles wasn't around to see that one,' she said, hoping the glib remark would diffuse the sexual tension.

For tonight at least.

It was far too early in the planning stages to be throwing herself at Nick in the hope that he'd relieve her of her virginity.

Nick's reply was a growled comment she didn't catch, but something in his slow steps as they crossed the car park towards where he'd left the car suggested he was having second thoughts about inviting her back to his place.

'And as he isn't around, there's no need for us to eat together,' she added. 'You could drop me home.'

He stopped and turned towards her and for a moment she thought he was going to kiss her again.

Hoped?

Yes—but there was a tremor of fear there as well.

She was definitely swimming in dangerous waters.

She looked up at him but was unable to see his expression, his face in shadow, his eyes hidden by the darkness.

'I know you keep bringing up Charles in these conversations, but is that all your scheming little heart is considering here?' he demanded.

'*My* scheming little heart?' she said, hoping indignation would hide the spurt of fear flickering in her body. 'I like that, when it was your idea in the first place.'

'So you keep reminding me, sweet Phoebe,' he said dryly. 'Yet I can't help feeling you're playing some deeper game. And don't try that innocent ''who me'' look on me. I've three sisters who've been using it for years, and I can tell you it no longer works.'

He paused for a heartbeat then added, 'Though it's never before prompted an urge to kiss it away.'

This kiss surpassed the earlier one, fiery tendrils of sensation coiling around Phoebe's heart and clutching at her lungs. They spread like liquid fire into every corner of her body, heating the tissues to a white-hot need she felt but couldn't understand.

Desire?

Attraction?

Lust?

His lips moved against hers, murmuring what might have been endearments, and his arms folded her tightly against his body. She felt the bones of his chest hard against her breasts, felt her nipples pucker with an aching need. Was this what her father had felt?

So many times…

Phoebe sprang back, angry with herself for what she saw as weakness, though wondering too about attraction and need, lust and love.

Sanity prevailed, and she edged further away.

'I'm really not hungry,' she said, still surprised by the truth of this excuse. 'I think I'd rather go home.'

Nick said nothing, though he studied her for a moment, then put out his hand to smooth her hair before unlocking his car and holding the door open for her. But when he turned out of the car park, he headed for her place, not down the road to where he lived.

She glanced towards him, hoping to read his mood, but his profile, with its high forehead, straight nose and jutting, determined chin gave nothing away.

Relief and disappointment warred in Phoebe's breast, but relief was definitely the stronger of the two emotions. After all, she needed time to consider her reactions to Nick's kisses—and even more time to think about the long-term implications of a one-night stand with her boss!

This was not an exercise to be undertaken lightly.

Another glance at that firm profile caused a new feathering of sensation down her spine.

Dangerous ground.

Her immediate concern was to find something to talk about to distract her from his closeness—and her own subversive thoughts. She remembered Peter Carter's distress.

'Will you get permission to try the treatment on Jackie?'

Nick glanced her way then turned his attention back to the road. He nodded as if he understood what she was doing—and accepted it.

'I would think so,' he said slowly. 'But it's not likely to be granted until all other avenues have been pursued.'

Something in his voice told her he disapproved of this approach.

'Do you think it will be too late by then?' she guessed, and saw his shoulders lift and heard the exhalation of a deep sigh.

'Specialists have been using surgery followed by radiation and chemo for decades now. They've used radiation to reduce the size of tumours prior to surgery, and come up with variations of the drugs used, and different combinations of drugs, and these have shown some good results. Alfa-interferon, which is a natural protein used to produce a cancer inhibiting protein in unaffected cells, has had the best results to date. On cases caught early, it works, but on cases where the disease has already spread to other organs in the body there's a very low success rate whatever the drug regime followed.'

She absorbed the explanation, at the same time inwardly admiring his ability to separate his emotional involvement with Peter from his scientific rationale of the cancer that was killing his friend.

An ability she'd do well to emulate, considering part of her had been reacting to any change of cadence in his voice as he spoke.

'So you're saying try the new treatment early?'

'Why not?' he demanded. 'At the moment, we're only allowed to try it on a handful of patients. With Peter, it was approved because, as a scientist himself, he understood it was experimental. One of the arguments the ethicists will use against Jackie having it early is that she's so young.'

'She's eighteen now, nearly nineteen, and melanoma is like breast cancer,' Phoebe protested. 'It seems to attack young people much more aggressively than older patients. Surely that's enough reason for us to treat it just as aggressively.'

She saw his lips twist into a rueful smile.

'You'd think so, wouldn't you?'

Phoebe said nothing, thinking instead of the implications of the treatment, wondering why ethics committees might have trouble with the concept.

'But it's virtually no treatment at all,' she protested. 'I mean, all you're doing is taking some tumour cells from the patient, allowing them to multiply outside the body, then injecting them back in, in the hope they'll trigger the patient's own immune system into rejecting them and then rejecting all the similar cells already in his or her body.'

'Autoimmunity!' Nick murmured, bringing the car to a halt outside her cottage. 'You'd think it would be the treatment of choice, but, like all new methods of treatment, it has to be proven in clinical trials before being generally accepted for use.'

He paused then added, 'Though speaking of immunity, shall we get back off medical subjects and see how yours is holding up?'

Phoebe turned in her seat and stared at him. He must file every little comment away in his computer-like brain, to have remembered her mentioning her immunity.

And as it wasn't holding up at all well, a fact which he must surely know, then sitting a second longer in this car was definitely not a good idea.

'Mine's great,' she lied, while her fingers fumbled for the doorhandle.

'It's over here,' Nick said, leaning across her so his body pressed against her breasts. 'That's if you're sure you want to go.'

'Quite s-sure!' Phoebe stammered, going hot all over as the words faltered from her lips. 'Don't bother getting out with me. I'll be fine. Save you locking the car.'

But he ignored her flow of excuses. Easing himself out of the car, he walked around the bonnet to hold the door as she stood up.

He escorted her down her path, beside her but not touching, took the key from her now nerveless fingers and opened the front door for her.

Then, while she waited uncertainly for his next move, half hoping and half dreading he'd come in, he bowed a funny little bow and said, 'Goodnight, sweet Phoebe.'

And walked away without a backward glance.

CHAPTER SEVEN

PHOEBE slept badly and blamed the fact she'd missed dinner, but she certainly hadn't been hungry when Nick had dropped her home. Disappointed in a way, but not hungry.

She woke to bright sunshine, but closed her eyes against its yellow glow. Far too cheerful a day when her mind was confused and her body restless. Rain would have been better.

A deluge.

Floods.

Tidal waves.

The shrill ring of the phone cut short her ruminations, which had switched from the actual weather to weather-like comparisons of her runaway emotions.

'Phoebe? Are you up and about? Free for a couple of hours today? The Americans have heard about our Beach Watch Programme and want to see us at work. Charles is…'

The sudden pause in Nick's explanations gave Phoebe time to recapture the breath the sound of his voice had stolen.

'Busy!' he finished. 'Considering they'll have TV cameras and a reporter on the beach, I'd like to have two of us going through our paces.'

'TV cameras and a reporter?' She echoed the words that made the least sense to her.

'Having visiting experts here is far more interesting to our local media than having the same old faces pushing sun safety, but, regardless of why they're interested, this is a great opportunity not only for some publicity for the clinic but to spread the word.'

Phoebe nodded into the phone. Spreading the word that even limited sunbathing was dangerous was one of Nick's pet projects. It was why he'd initiated Beach Watch, using students and clinic staff to walk among the sunbathers on the popular local surfing beaches, distributing leaflets about sun safety and asking if people wanted a quick skin examination.

'Are you still there?' he demanded.

'Of course! I was just thinking.'

'Don't think, just say yes. Or are you busy? I didn't mean to push.'

Phoebe chuckled.

'Of course you meant to push. You did it to me back when I was a student—you push all the female students into helping you right through summer because you believe young men on the beach are far more likely to agree to a woman examining their skin.

'Not that I mind,' she added quickly, as early detection of possible danger signs gave her immense satisfaction.

'So you can come today? The camera crew will be there at eleven, but I thought—'

'As we were going to be on the beach any-way, we might as well do a patrol,' Phoebe finished for him.

He chuckled and she was pleased she'd made him laugh.

'You know me too well,' he told her, caus-ing a little trickle of excitement along her nerves as her wayward mind took the words another way. 'I'll drop by your place at about ten. That suit you?'

She nodded again, then realised he couldn't see her nod and managed a casual, 'Fine.'

Though it wasn't fine. It was stupid. Perhaps she should get this 'ending her virginity' thing right out of her mind, and revive her immunity to men like Nick. What would happen if she fell in love with him? Really in love?

Beyond whatever it was she was feeling now?

She'd be repeating her mother's mistake—that's what would happen. Reliving her mother's life with her father all over again.

But she wouldn't fall in love with him.

All these weird reactions were the result of a chemical attraction—a physical thing. Which made him the ideal candidate for The Plan!

A temporary lover. Like a locum. Filling in for a short time. That was all she wanted of Nick David.

These thoughts stayed with her as she showered, then dressed in what she thought of as her 'Beach Watch' outfit. A white bikini because it got hot on the beach even at the very beginning of the summer season, covered by loose white cotton harem trousers and a long-sleeved white cotton shirt, sheer enough to allow her skin to breathe but dense enough to combat most of the sun's lethal rays.

Even with the covering, she'd still apply sunscreen, and reapply it after swimming. There was no point in hammering home a sun-safe message to the general public then ignoring it yourself.

She was checking the contents of her beach bag when the doorbell announced Nick's arrival.

'Aha! Phoebe clad in virginal white! Wasn't the original Phoebe a goddess of some kind? Was she a virgin?'

Phoebe clutched the door frame for support.

Damn the man! Was he tuned into her thoughts? She battled the heat she knew was heading for her cheeks, and bent her head over her large beach-bag in case she lost.

'She was the moon goddess, if you must know,' she muttered at him, then glanced up as his low chuckle tripped a quiver down her spine.

She turned her attention back to the bag. Sunscreen, sunglasses—

'I knew there must have been a reason for kissing you in the car park last night. I couldn't figure if it was moon madness or Phoebe madness, and now you tell me they're one and the same thing.'

'Well, I'd hate to think it was because you found me attractive!' she told him tartly. 'Heaven forbid!'

'There's no moon now,' he murmured, and again she looked up from her pretended absorption with the beach-bag, this time to see blue eyes, dark with what looked like desire, studying her intently.

'Which is why we should be on our way to the beach,' she reminded him, deliberately misinterpreting his words in order to divert the conversation into safer channels.

She led the way out the door, leaving him to pull it shut behind them. He was as well covered as she was, but his casual trousers were of a natural linen fabric, his shirt a manly version of her own. Nubby linen, but woven loosely so the material did nothing to hide the contours of his chest or the sprinkling of dark hair on his chest and the suggestion of more, arrowing downward from his waist.

'Got your hat?' he asked, and she realised she'd been too caught up in the suggestive conversation to remember that basic sun-accessory. Found her keys in the bag and went back inside, grabbing the floppy-brimmed Panama off the hook inside the door then walking out again.

'How's Peter this morning?' she asked, by way of taking the conversation and her mind on to work-related topics.

'Much brighter,' Nick told her, but the gravity in his voice told her it was a temporary thing.

'Do you think his tumours are too widespread for this treatment to work?'

He shook his head, opened his car door for her and didn't answer until he, too, was seated in the car.

'It's working on some tumours and not on others,' he said. 'Trials in other hospitals have had similar results in their patients. The immune system seems to kick in to reduce the size of some of the tumours though why it is so selective we can't work out.'

He started the car and eased out from the kerb, his eyes on the road but the frown between his eyebrows suggesting his mind was elsewhere.

'But you're using cells from the patient's own tumours to trigger the response,' Phoebe said, trying to follow his train of thought. 'And as all the tumours are secondary as a result of melanoma, shouldn't they all have the same characteristics?'

'And respond in the same way?' Nick said, then he sighed and added, 'You'd think so, wouldn't you? That's why it's such a puzzle.'

'Could the tumours change in their nature or structure?'

Nick shrugged.

'They do to the extent that they are a proliferation of the cells of the particular organ where they form, but when you consider that every cell in the body has the same DNA configuration, then you would also assume they'd have the same response to this treatment.'

Phoebe relaxed and gave her mind to the problem. Discussing work with Nick always challenged her and now it was a welcome diversion.

'I suppose you've tried taking cells from the tumours that aren't reacting and using them for the next lot of treatment?'

Nick shot her a smile.

'Same negative result. Except that they seem to work less effectively overall and at a hundred and forty thousand dollars a shot we can't afford to play around too much.'

'It's an enormous expense,' Phoebe agreed, knowing all the variable costs from space in hospital labs to staff wages that were factored into this 'per treatment' accounting. 'So it makes sense to stick to what works.'

'Does it?' Nick demanded. 'That's what's really bugging me at the moment. Do we put our resources into something that has some results, or go all out to find the final answer? It's got to be there somewhere.'

'Someone certainly has to be looking further ahead,' Phoebe told him. 'But in the meantime we've got all the Peters and Jackies in the world. Surely they're entitled to a chance at what's already available.'

'Of course they are.' He had pulled up at traffic lights and now slammed his hand against the steering wheel as if the frustration he was feeling couldn't be put into words.

'Well, we can only do what we can,' Phoebe reminded him. 'By doing our beach patrols at least we have a chance of saving some poor soul from ending up where Peter and Jackie are now.'

The lights changed and the car rolled forward.

'First a mother hen and now a little ray of sunshine. You were wasted on Charles, young woman. Totally wasted.'

Phoebe glanced his way, assuming he was teasing her, but the look on his face was more grim than light-hearted, and she wondered whether his thoughts remained with Peter. Disturbed by the physical responses merely looking at him evoked, she turned her attention to the scenery beyond the car. Tree-lined streets were a much safer focus for her eyes.

Silence made Nick turn towards his companion. That darned white gear enhanced her dark beauty and for all the smart remarks he might make about moon goddesses or mother hens, he found himself thinking about Phoebe Moreton in ways he knew he shouldn't.

Kissing those full, sensual lips was bad enough, but imagining his lips on other parts of her body was insanity. She was definitely not a love 'em and leave 'em type of woman, and right now—at least until his commitment to Peter was over—he had no time to give to any other form of relationship.

Yet, since that first—undoubtedly foolish, but totally indescribable—kiss in the corridor it was as if she'd got into his blood, and now every time he saw her his body reacted in a way it had never reacted before.

To any woman!

He put it down to lust but that bothered him even more. Some strait-laced part of his mind told him it was wrong to feel such an earthy emotion for a woman like Phoebe. It was somehow indecent.

Which didn't stop his body reacting to her presence in a way that made wearing such loose-fitting trousers practically compulsory. Hopefully, she wouldn't see through their weave to the swimming trunks which had suddenly become too tight.

'Divide the available resources or get more money?'

He realised she must have been talking for some time while he'd pursued his dark thoughts. She'd ended with a question—but what question?

'Use some funds for development of new treatments and the rest for the clinical trials already under way?' He took a stab at what she'd asked. 'I'm tempted to suggest that to the board but it limits the amount available in both spheres and lessens the impact of the research. More money is the answer, but finding donors takes time and effort and a lot of follow-through work.'

He shook his head.

'I've been willing to put in the effort, but time's another thing. Some days it seems all we do is steal from Peter to pay Paul.'

Speaking about money reminded him of what he'd meant to tell her earlier in the week.

'I met——' he began, then Phoebe screamed, and out of the corner of his eye he saw the small figure of a child darting into the road. He slammed on the brakes, and spun the wheel to pull the car away from that direction. They jolted to a halt as the bonnet hit a car coming towards them. He heard the dull thunk as Phoebe's head connected with the window, but when he turned towards her she was already struggling to release her seat belt. Anxious to get out—no doubt to find the child.

'Are you OK?' he asked, but she was half-way out of the car and didn't answer. He tried to release his own door, found it was jammed and eased over to the passenger side to get out that way.

A woman knelt beside the car, her arms around a little boy who was yelling lustily. Phoebe was squatting beside the pair, soothing both the panicky mother and the youngster.

'He's not hurt. You swerved in time to miss him,' she said, apparently sensing his presence and looking up with a radiant smile. 'Are the people in the other car all right?'

Nick blinked away the effect of that smile and turned to where the driver of the other vehicle was emerging. The flush on his face suggested he either suffered very high blood pressure or was in a towering rage. Perhaps both.

'What do you think you were doing?' he bellowed at Nick. 'Look at my car! See the damage you've done? What are you—drunk or something?'

'Probably something,' Nick said, leaving Phoebe with the cause of the accident and walking towards the man to head him off before he vented his anger on the already overwrought mother. 'I'm sorry about your car. I'll give you my insurance details. I swerved to avoid a child and you were unlucky enough to be in the way.'

'Where? What child?' the man demanded, and at that moment Phoebe stood up, the little boy in her arms, the mother busy picking up things she'd dropped from her bag as she darted into the street.

'That child,' Nick said, pointing towards the scene.

'But that's Jamie. That's my grandchild. We were to meet them at the beach. Who's that woman holding him? Where's my daughter?'

Nick shook his head. He saw no reason to keep answering the man's demanding questions, especially as a police car had now pulled up and he'd be asked far more pertinent ones by them.

'Perhaps you should go to your daughter,' Nick told the man. 'She's had a shock.'

The stranger shot him one more angry glare then bustled away, and Nick could hear his voice berating his daughter before he even reached her.

Then something he'd said earlier replayed itself in Nick's head. 'We' were meeting them at the beach. Who was we?

He glanced towards the car, and saw a woman slumped back in the passenger seat. Concerned onlookers had opened the door and were peering anxiously in, but, no doubt aware of the advice to not move people before assessing injuries, no one had lifted her out.

Nick nodded to the policeman who was approaching purposefully, then waved his hand towards the second car.

'I'll answer all your questions in a moment,' he said, 'but first I'd like to check the passenger over there. I'm a doctor,' he added, then moved through the parting crowd, the policeman at his heels.

The woman was in her late fifties or early sixties, dressed for the beach in a long blue shift.

Her lips were almost as blue as the dress and Nick knew she hadn't painted them that colour.

'Heart attack by the look of things,' Nick said to the policeman. 'Could you call an ambulance, and tell them they'll need resuscitation equipment?'

He bent over and breathed into the woman's mouth, pumping air from his lungs into hers. She needed cardiac massage as well and, having given her six breaths, he directed the policeman to help as he lifted her out of the car and laid her on the ground.

'There's no time to worry about exacerbating other injuries,' he explained. 'I'll do the CPR while you keep the crowd back. Make sure there's a clear path for the ambulance.'

He could hear the siren approaching and hoped it would arrive in time to revive the woman before too much damage had been done. Intent on his task, he counted, pumped and breathed, stopping only when an ambulance attendant pushed him aside.

'We'll take care of her now, sir,' the man said, then he did a classic double take and added, 'Dr David! Didn't recognise you. How long's she been like this?'

Nick gave his best estimation while the two attendants set up the electric current which, hopefully, would shock the woman's heart back into action. Then he looked around, wondering where the woman's husband was. Surely he'd noticed his wife's condition, and even if he hadn't, he must by now have seen the emergency services' activity around his car.

He caught a glimpse of the angry man on the far footpath, the little boy on one arm and his free hand waving in the air as he obviously continued to berate his daughter.

A flash of white told Nick Phoebe was also there. Trust her to stick by the woman as moral support.

'Heart's beating,' one of the attendants said. 'We'll load her now. Do we know who she is? Has she someone with her?'

'There's a chap who's probably her husband. I'll get him,' Nick volunteered, and he made his way around the smashed cars and the greedily assembling tow trucks to the footpath opposite.

He saw the relief in Phoebe's eyes as he approached and smiled at her. Then frowned. She was as white as her clothes and a trickle of bright blood lay like a scar across her right temple.

He curbed the instinctive need to hold her and examine her injuries—and yell at her for not sitting down and taking care of herself—and turned to the man.

'They're loading your passenger into the ambulance. The hospital will need details,' he said.

The young woman wailed 'Mum!' then dashed away, but the man wasn't going to show such weakness.

'What do you mean, loading her into an ambulance? Why does *she* need an ambulance? Nothing wrong with her.'

He made it sound as if only he—or perhaps men—had the right to emergency services, but Nick ignored his peeve and explained.

'I think she's had a heart attack. If you want to travel to the hospital with her, the police can contact you there if they need to speak to you.'

The man's face grew even more flushed and he thrust the child back into Phoebe's arms and stepped aggressively towards Nick.

'The police won't want to speak to me!' he roared, spluttering with rage. 'It was your fault, this accident. All your fault.'

Fortunately, the young woman returned, grabbed her child and turned towards her father.

'They're taking Mum to the Southern Cross. If you want a lift you'll have to come now. Leave your name and address with this man and he can give it to the tow truck people and the police.'

The man stared at his daughter as if she'd suddenly turned into an alien.

'Come on, Dad,' she said, her voice gentler now. 'Mum needs you at the hospital.'

'Never needed me in her life,' the man blustered, but he did dig into his hip pocket and produce a wallet. Still muttering to himself, he took out a card and handed it to Nick.

'If I lose my no-claim bonus over this you'll have to pay it,' he warned, then he let his daughter lead him away.

'Charming fellow,' Phoebe murmured, then, as Nick turned towards her, she gave a little sigh and slid gracefully to the footpath.

She'd recovered almost before she reached the ground, enough to protest volubly when he tried to make her lie down.

'No way!' she said. 'I'm OK now. It must have been the shock. Truly, Nick, I'm fine.'

She shook off his restraining hand and sat up on the kerb, propping her head in her hands and breathing deeply.

'How stupid!' she muttered crossly, more to herself than to him. 'Swooning like some eighteenth-century virgin!'

Then, as the words hung in the air between them, he caught a mounting tide of pink sweeping into her cheeks, and as she glanced up to see if he'd heard he read confusion and something else—embarrassment, possibly?—in her eyes.

'I'll take you home,' he said, his voice gruff with an emotion he didn't want to analyse.

'No way!' she said, repeating her earlier refusal. 'We're here to do a Beach Watch. I know I look a bit grubby but I don't think anyone will notice.'

Then she pointed to his car. 'Not that you'll be taking anyone anywhere in that, I shouldn't think.'

She reached up to touch her temple, reminding Nick to check the wound.

'Is there blood?' she asked him. 'Could you mop it up? And when the TV people arrive, you'd better be the one on camera. Seeing a battered Beach Watch doctor might make people wonder exactly what goes on in the programme.'

She smiled at him, apparently over her earlier confusion, but the smile made his reactions worse. He produced his handkerchief and dabbed at the graze, his fingers trembling as he realised how close she'd come to being more seriously hurt.

The urge to hold her in his arms and protect her—possibly for ever—was so strong he was shaken by the awesome implications of such feelings. Was it time to reconsider his priorities? Time to—

'Hey, guys! Sorry you couldn't make it last night, but at least you're here to show us what you do on this Beach Watch thing.'

Phoebe struggled to her feet as Brad Moss and Bill Cotter appeared beside them, dead-heating with the policeman who obviously had a few questions to ask Nick.

'I'll take the visitors down to the beach,' she told Nick, knowing he'd be unable to stop her under the circumstances.

He'd been standing frowning out towards the ocean, but when she spoke he turned to face her, blinking as if trying to remember who she was.

'You shouldn't go,' he told her, before turning to Bill to add, 'Keep an eye on her, would you? We've had a slight accident and Phoebe hit her head. She shouldn't be here at all, but who can tell a woman what she should or shouldn't do?'

He frowned at Phoebe in case she'd missed his disapproval of her intransigence, then turned to the impatient policeman.

Bill seemed to feel 'keeping an eye on her' included taking her arm and staying close by her side. Having already been impolite enough to miss the dinner with the visitors, Phoebe felt she couldn't protest and let herself be led across the road to the beach.

'I guess we should wait for the camera crew,' she said. 'Nick and I had hoped to do a sweep of the beach before they arrived but, what with running into cars and women having heart attacks, there really isn't time.'

She detached herself from Bill's clasp to dig into her shoulder-bag.

'These are the leaflets we hand out,' she said, producing the brightly printed sheets which not only warned of the dangers of UV rays but gave the exposure level at different numbers on the UV index.

'Our local news broadcasts on radio and TV always include the UV index number in their weather reports, and see the flashing number over there...'

She pointed towards the lifesavers' watch tower where the number six was flashing.

'That's today's UV index, which indicates a moderate exposure level. Our other warning to people is to not stay out in the sun between ten in the morning and two in the afternoon, when the UV radiation is at its highest.'

'We have similar warnings in our coastal towns, but in landlocked areas it's more difficult to get the message across,' Brad told her. 'Folk tend to connect skin cancer with the beach. Telling a farmer he should wear sun-glasses and cover up isn't so easy. Telling him not to work between ten and two would be downright impossible.'

Phoebe nodded.

'Same here, and long-distance truck drivers are another problem. Try convincing them to wear a long-sleeved shirt when their ''truckies' uniform'' consists of shorts and a black sin-glet! When a man comes in with significant sun damage to his right arm, we know he's spent a lifetime on the road.'

'It's concise enough, yet with information like the index thing which people might want to keep.' Bill was reading through the leaflet. 'Less likely to exacerbate the litter problem.'

'We had that argument with the local coun-cil when we first began handing them out. Now we ask people if they want to keep it or if they would just like to read it while we check their skin. That way, if they don't want it they can give it back. I think most Australians are litter conscious now, so it hasn't been a major problem.'

'Yet!'

Nick's voice startled Phoebe and she turned to see him smiling down at her, while behind him a tow truck carried his damaged vehicle away.

'You couldn't drive it?' she said, although she'd guessed as much when she'd seen the extent of the damage.

'Only because the front panel and bumper bar had been pushed in and were scrunched up against the wheel. We tried to free it but even if we had, the wheels were likely to be out of alignment. Best to get it fixed.'

He was speaking of such an ordinary matter—the aftermath of the accident—but his voice had developed a power to physically affect her, so mundane words like 'wheel' and 'alignment' caused a fluttery sensation in her skin. She turned towards the ocean, staring out at its vastness, with its rolling lines of surf, as she tried to regain control of her body.

Perhaps if she put the virginity thing right out of her mind, life would return to normal.

'Do you want the cameras to catch that blank expression?' Nick asked.

She swung back to face him, then looked beyond him to the approaching cameraman.

'I was thinking. That was a pensive look!' she retorted. 'And I've already told you. No cameras. Look at me. I'm filthy. You do the talking, Dr David. After all, you're the boss.'

'Yes, I am,' he said, his smile now causing more problems than his voice. 'Though you only seem to remember that when it's convenient.'

She drew in breath to argue but fortunately Brad intervened.

'How about you and Bill do the leaflet distribution, Phoebe, while Nick and I do the interview.'

He winked at Nick and added, 'I think Bill would like to get to know your colleague a whole lot better.'

And although she didn't really want to walk along the beach with Bill attached to her arm like an unnecessary accessory, it was a good excuse to escape Nick's immediate vicinity and the problems it caused.

She smiled at Bill, let him take her arm to steady her while she slipped off her sandals and dropped them into her bag, then she walked with him down the steps and onto the warm golden sands—resisting the urge to look back.

CHAPTER EIGHT

NICK watched them depart then turned a false smile in the direction of the cameraman who was lugging his gear along the footpath. It had been a long time since the local press had run a story on the Beach Watch programme, and with the advent of summer the exposure would be timely.

So he had to forget how seeing Phoebe with Bill made him feel and push the sun-safe message to the media, and through them to the general public.

'I insisted they give me the job when I learnt the hunky boss himself was going to be present. Who's your friend?'

Nick grinned at the reporter, who'd appeared from a different direction. Linda Wilson was a one-time date of his, one of his 'window-dressing' blondes.

'Brad Moss, meet Linda Wilson.'

He introduced the pair, smiling more broadly when the American's courtly manners sparked Linda's interest.

'Tell me why you're out here,' Linda said to the visitor. 'Surely the USA has extensive sun-safe programmes.'

'We do,' Brad agreed. 'But Queensland leads the world in research, as well as preventative initiatives, so it's a logical place for skin cancer specialists to visit.'

'Leads the world in the occurrence of skin cancer as well,' Nick reminded him. 'Look at those people sunbathing. Recent research tells us that two in five adults admit to lying around in the sun, in spite of all the warnings they've been given. And while nine out of ten parents say they don't let their children outside without sunscreen, only six out of ten apply it to their own skin when they go outdoors.'

'Are these the latest figures?' Linda asked, and Nick nodded, although his attention was on a white-clad figure strolling along the beach, arm in arm with a tall, blond, good-looking American male.

'I'll fax you the survey,' he added, telling himself the squelchy feeling in his gut couldn't possibly be jealousy. More likely to be concern for a colleague who'd recently fainted.

'Do these figures correspond with your research?' Linda turned her attention back to

Brad, who rattled off some statistics from his university's cancer research centre.

'What about prevention?' she asked him. 'Here we hand out hats, sunscreen and easy-to-understand information to all children in their first year of school, and we've pro-grammes like this as follow-up. Is a similar early-education programme in place in the US?'

Brad began to explain about the state-to-state differences in health programmes and Nick tuned out. Phoebe and Bill had stopped their perambulations, and Phoebe was exam-ining the skin of a tall, stringy, red-headed teenager.

'There's an example of someone who shouldn't ever be on a beach,' he said to Linda, pointing to where Bill was now exam-ining the lad's skin. 'Not without any covering on his legs, arms or torso.'

As they all watched, Phoebe glanced up, and when she saw Nick she waved her hand. He felt a clenching of a different kind in his ab-domen and, excusing himself to the media crew and Brad, he took the steps two at a time and crossed the sand towards them.

'What do you think?' Phoebe asked, when Nick arrived at the group. Then she must have remembered her manners, for she added, 'I'm sorry. Phil, this is Dr Nick David. Nick, this is Phil. He said he's been meaning to get someone to check this mark on his neck.'

Phoebe indicated the mark, a dark blue-brown splotch with untidy edges, and a swollen pinkness on its lower limit.

'How long has it been there?' Nick asked, and the young man shrugged.

'Maybe a couple of months. Might always have had something there. I'm a freckly kind of person, so what's one more freckle?'

He spoke with the casual offhandedness of his generation, but Nick sensed it was a cover for deep concern. So many people put off having visible or tactile signs of trouble investigated because they feared the diagnosis. They didn't *want* to know they have a problem.

'I'd like you to come in to the clinic on Monday,' he said, hoping brisk matter-of-factness would ease the lad's worry. 'Here's my card. It has the clinic's address on it. You can give me a ring some time over the weekend if you want to talk about it, or your parents can phone me if they wish. If I'm not at home,

I'll make arrangements for all calls to be transferred to my mobile.'

'You're operating on Monday,' Phoebe reminded him.

Nick frowned then nodded, turning again to the young man.

'I won't be in the clinic but I'll warn my colleague, Charles Marlowe, to expect you. He'll explain all the procedures to you.'

Phoebe could see the tension in Phil's face and feel it in the muscles beneath his skin, but he put on a show of bravado.

'Well, that's put a dampener on our day at the beach,' he said. 'I guess you're going to tell me I should get out of the sun right now?'

'I don't think I have to tell you that,' Nick said, and the three of them were about to move on when the reporter arrived.

One of Nick's blondes!

Phoebe managed a smile and hoped it looked OK, although an edgy uneasiness churned her stomach when she imagined the pair of them together.

'Have you found something bad? Could we film the patient and follow up on him? On his diagnosis and treatment?' the blonde asked brightly.

Without thinking, Phoebe moved forward to shield Phil from the camera.

'It's a spot that needs checking out—nothing more,' she said. 'And although he's not yet a patient, there is such a thing as patient privacy and confidentiality.'

'But it would make a great story,' Linda persisted, turning to Nick for support. 'Especially if it's malignant and the clinic cures him. Just think of the good publicity for your cause.'

Phoebe glared at the woman, stepping closer to her because she didn't want Phil to hear the argument, but before she could get really stuck into Linda for her insensitivity Nick intervened, taking Linda by the arm and leading her away.

Fortunately the cameraman and Brad followed, and Phoebe was left with the shocked young man and Bill, who was hovering solicitously over her, not their patient.

'It may not be anything to worry about,' she told Phil. 'Even if it is malignant, if we get it early we can cure it. So don't spend the whole weekend fretting over what might be.'

Phil smiled at her.

'Easier said than done?'

'Of course it is,' Bill told him. 'It's one of the worst things about doctors—they always sound so know-it-all when they tell patients not to worry. Give them a suspicious spot on the neck and see how *they* feel.'

It must have been the right approach, for Phil laughed, then bent down to gather up his things. The young woman with him was looking shocked, and a little scared, and Phoebe felt her heart ache for the teenagers, whose perfect day at the beach had been ruined by the shadowy threat of cancer.

'No matter how often we tell them cancer's just a word, not a death threat, it doesn't sink in, does it?' Bill murmured.

'I guess they know that in many cases it might be a death threat,' Phoebe reminded him. 'Though eventually, and maybe sooner rather than later, it won't be.'

They continued along the beach, distributing leaflets and stopping to speak to people, examining skin when asked and generally spreading the word. At some stage the cameraman came up and took long shots of them, which Phoebe guessed would be used to set the scene with voice-over from either the reporter or Nick. Depressed by their discovery, she was beyond worrying about how dirty she might look, so she stuck doggedly to her task, criss-crossing the sand and trying to convince people to take better care of their skin.

'Brad has a hire car. He's suggested we all lunch together then he'll drop us home.' Nick was waiting for them when they returned to the steps.

Bill seconded this idea with far too much enthusiasm, but Phoebe's head was aching and she guessed Nick would prefer to be at the hospital.

'I'm too sweaty and dirty to be seen in public—well, anywhere but on the beach.' She smiled an apology at Brad. 'So if you'd excuse me, I might hop into a cab and head home for a restful afternoon.'

'We could take you home to shower and change, then go on to lunch,' Bill suggested, but Phoebe shook her head.

'No, really. I've had enough excitement for one day.'

Nick was frowning at her, but it was too bad if he thought she should accept the invitation. She'd already given up enough of her Saturday to his pet scheme, and there was no way she was going to spend more time with him until she'd had time to analyse all the new, unsettling reactions she was suffering when with him.

And given more thought to The Plan.

'I'll take you home,' he said, surprising her by how far out her reading of his reaction had been. He turned to Brad. 'You're here for a few more days. I'll make some other time for us to get together.'

Then he lifted his arm and a taxi appeared as if by magic, the driver's obvious impatience at holding up a stream of traffic leading to a minimum of farewells.

'You look as sick as a dog!' Nick scolded, when they were both belted into the rear seat and he'd given the driver her address. 'That was sheer stupidity, walking up and down the beach when you obviously weren't feeling well. Why on earth didn't you go home earlier? Or was it that over-friendly American's company that kept you there?'

His anger caught Phoebe by surprise, then it sparked her own.

'Well, thanks for the compliment!' she retorted. 'For your information, I also *feel* as sick as a dog, so if you've any sense at all you'll sit there and shut up so I can concentrate on not throwing up all over you.'

'Hell! Do you feel that bad? Do you want the cab to stop?'

He reached over and put an arm around her shoulders—difficult, given the restrictions of two seat belts—then drew her awkwardly towards him.

She pushed away, knowing that being close to him was dangerous. Besides, her anger was still burning.

'Actually, I didn't feel sick until we were waiting on the pavement. Maybe it was the mention of lunch.'

Which was odd, given her partiality for food. She leaned her head back against the corner of the cab and tried to figure out this other, and far more puzzling, new phenomenon.

The cab drew up outside her home. Behind a shiny dark green Jaguar which had obviously just arrived.

'Oh, no! Not a fatherly visit today of all days!' she muttered to herself.

At the same time Nick said, 'Isn't that your father?'

Before she could ask how he could recognise her father, the man himself was there, opening the cab door, greeting her with his usual enthusiasm and helping her out of the cab.

'Ah, Nick! Good to see you again,' her father added, leaning past her into the back seat to shake hands with Nick. 'You coming in?'

'No, he isn't!' Phoebe said, forcing her father out of the way and slamming the door shut in case Nick had other ideas. 'He has patients to visit,' she added rather lamely, when the startled expression in her father's eyes told her she'd been extremely rude.

Fortunately, Nick must have got the message for the cab drew away from the curb and continued on down the street.

'Just thought I'd pop in and see my best girl. How are you, darling?' Michael Moreton said.

As he was talking, Phoebe asked him, 'How do you know Nick David?'

Her father chuckled.

'Who'll answer first? You or me?'

'I'm fine—there, that's me done,' she said, leading the way up the path and unlocking the door. 'Now it's your turn.'

She spoke abruptly, but a wild guess at her father's reply was churning her already unsettled stomach.

'He came to see me last week. Part of his plan to tempt business into sponsoring medical programmes. Edward Sheilds put him on to me.'

There was a pause and Phoebe, who'd been hanging up her hat on the stand inside the door, turned enquiringly towards him.

'And?' she prompted.

'Well, I thought he'd have mentioned it to you by now but he obviously hasn't worked out the finer details.'

Her father started his usual practice of pacing as he spoke—up and back across a rich red Turkish rug he'd given her when she'd bought the little cottage.

'What finer details, Dad? And stop moving. Look at me.'

He turned towards her, a dark-haired, well-built man, at fifty-four still impossibly good-looking.

'We talked about this business of you not being able to begin your specialist studies while you're in that unit. Of not being able to count that time towards your dermatology experience.'

Phoebe wondered if the top of the human head could blow off with rage. Hers certainly felt as if it might go at any moment.

'Dad! How could you discuss my career with someone else—without my permission? And who said I wanted to specialise? I've been telling you for years that I was pretty sure all I wanted to do was GP work. This skin-cancer thing is just an added string to my bow when I eventually apply for a position in a practice. Just what were the two of you planning? Was Nick David going to pull strings and in return get a healthy donation from you?'

She took a turn across the carpet herself. 'No wonder people were making cryptic remarks. I guess everyone knew about this but me. Just wait until I get my hands on that man!'

'But, darling,' Michael said, moving towards her with his hands outheld in a placating manner. 'You've always been ambitious. Of all my children, you're the one most like me. You want to be the best, to rise to the top, and specialising is the way to go to get there.'

Phoebe sighed, the spurt of anger dying as the full realisation of what he'd said sank in.

'Dad,' she said, waving him to a chair and sinking into one herself, 'I hate to disillusion you but I'm probably the least like you of all your children. I have next to no ambition. I did medicine because Mum felt I should use the brains I was given, and because I enjoy helping people. Now I'm a doctor, but nothing's changed. As far as I'm concerned, helping people at the basic, general-practice level is what I want to do. At least, that's my thinking at the moment.'

'But it's a dead end,' her father protested.

'Nonsense!' Phoebe told him. 'A GP sees new challenges every day, and has to continue to study and learn because he needs a far wider range of medical knowledge than any specialist.'

'And that's all you want?'

The incredulity in her father's voice was so strong Phoebe had to laugh. Not that Nick's involvement in this mad scheme had any humour in it. Although it did explain why he'd been so obliging with the making-Charles-jealous farce. Sweetening her up as a way of getting her father's donation.

The acidic bite of disappointment made her feel ill again, and she had to breathe deeply to counteract its poisonous effect.

Her father, apparently realising the futility of his argument, was now expounding on Matthew's studies in information technology. Phoebe managed the appropriate noises of approval, knowing Matthew, her half-brother from her father's third marriage, had inherited the drive and ambition she lacked. Though only in his first year at university, he was already running a small web page design company.

'Did you know Celeste is pregnant again? This baby is due in February.'

Phoebe nodded. Celeste was the first child of marriage number two, nearest to her in age, and earning Brownie points from their father for *her* ambition, which, as far as Phoebe could tell, was to add to the world's over-population problem.

'If all you're going to do is GP work, perhaps it's time you started thinking of marriage and a family.'

'Would you like a cup of coffee, Dad?' Phoebe said, as she felt her eyes crossing and the top of her head about to blow again. Better to get him coffee than throw a pot-plant at him.

'Do you have fresh beans? Do you use the grinder I gave you?'

Perhaps she should have thrown the pot-plant at him after all, she decided as she stalked off to the kitchen without dignifying his question with a reply.

But there was no escape. He followed her, working down through her numerous half-siblings and extolling their excellence in their schooling and extra-curricular activities.

Phoebe ground the beans—fresh—and made coffee, then dug through her store cupboard for a tin of biscuits he'd once given her and offered them to him.

He perched on a stool in the kitchen, and continued to relay the family news.

'And Beatrice's piano teacher tells us we have a genius on our hands.'

'She's only three, Dad. Don't push her.'

He looked offended by this remark, but fortunately the doorbell rang and Phoebe excused herself to answer it. Probably a couple of religious visitors of some denomination. She'd invite them in for coffee and let them do their spiel in front of her father. That should distract his attention from her future—and her lack of what he considered ambition.

'I was worried about you. About a delayed reaction—from the head injury or shock. I visited Peter but I was too distracted to do any more than depress him, so I came to see you for myself.'

Nick managed to deliver all this information in a single breathless run of words. The pace added to a suggestion of uncertainty about this usually positive man.

At any other time she might have felt sympathy for him, but today he was the epicentre of her problems.

'How dare you use me to get money from my father? Plotting with him to get me into the specialist programme, which, I'll have you know, is the last place I want to be. You may think specialising is the ultimate in life, but for your information I have other plans for my future so go away and stay away.'

She then slammed the door in his face and stalked back to the kitchen.

Her back quivered with nerves on full alert for another peal of the doorbell, but none came. She wasn't sure if that made her feel better or worse, but until her father left she wouldn't be able to untangle the snarl of different emotions she was feeling, and get her mind back to normality.

'Someone selling something?' her father asked.

'Something like that!' she replied.

Her father left shortly afterwards and her main concern, now she'd settled down enough to think straight, was that she had slammed the door in her boss's face. Although the silly carryings-on of the past week might have shifted her perspective of Nick David, the fact remained he was just that—her boss!

So, what did she do?

Phone him and apologise?

But shouldn't he be the one apologising? Talking to her father behind her back? Discussing her career as if she had no say in it? Using his connection with her to get his precious unit a donation?

By the time she reached this question, any idea of phoning to apologise flew out the window. It would be a cold day in hell before she spoke to him again.

About anything but work, she amended to herself as she stripped off her clothes and stepped into a hot shower.

But as she soaped her body she remembered how his kisses made her feel, and regret that she'd never know what it was like to make love with him niggled within her.

'Never know what it's like to make love with anyone, the rate you're going!' she muttered crossly to herself. 'Talk about a dunderhead! You can't even get yourself seduced successfully!'

By late afternoon she was in such a dither that when the doorbell rang again, she considered pretending to be out. Perhaps if she peeked through the window first...

'It's Jess, Phoebe. If you're in there, open up.'

Puzzled by Jess's assumption that she might be pretending to be out, Phoebe opened the door.

Jess pushed past her into the entry.

'Well, you look OK,' she said, 'though that dressing gown you're wearing looks way past its use-by date, especially if you're going to greet people wearing it.'

'I've had a shower and soon I'm going to bed,' Phoebe told her, then realised her mistake when Jess looked at her watch.

'At five o'clock in the afternoon. You *must* be sick. Nick told me about the accident and asked me to check on you. Any headache, blurry vision? What else would head-injured patients have?'

'Too many visitors!' Phoebe snapped. 'I'm a doctor so I do know about head-injury symptoms and you can tell Dr David I'm fine.'

Jess held up her hands in mock surrender.

'Hey! Don't get upset with me. I'm only doing an old pal a favour.'

She paused, eyeing Phoebe quizzically for a moment, then added, 'And speaking of my old pal, just what have you done to get him so tied up in knots? He came roaring around to my place in a brand new Mercedes he'd apparently borrowed from some car-dealer friend, mumbling some totally incomprehensible gibberish about car accidents and doors slamming in his face. What did you do? Turn down a date with him? That's about all I can imagine that would dent his ego.'

'He's upset over Peter,' Phoebe reminded her, refusing to believe anything she'd done, even slamming a door in his face, could have affected Nick.

'I guess so,' Jess said, but she continued to study her hostess. 'Has he told his mother about you?'

Phoebe sighed.

'Maybe I do have a head injury,' she said. 'A lot of this conversation—that bit in partic-ular—makes no sense. Peter said much the same thing to Nick yesterday. What on earth do I have to do with Nick's mother?'

Jess grinned at her.

'He always tells his mother about the women he dates—even me, although we never had a real date, more a convenience thing.'

'Well, there you go,' Phoebe countered. 'Proof there's nothing going on between me and Nick. When Peter asked him if he'd told his mother, he was most adamant in his de-nial.'

'Hmm!' Jess said, and Phoebe, who didn't like the sound of that neutral expression, changed the subject, asking Jess about her plans for the evening.

Which didn't, she learned, include Charles.

'So what's happened?' Phoebe asked, and Jess grinned at her.

'I've told him I won't go out with him again until he makes a decision about Anne's place in his life. I pointed out that if Anne seriously needs his help, then both of us—if there is to be an us—should go to her and help her.'

The simplicity of the solution made Phoebe smile.

'Good for you!' she said. 'And what was his reaction to that?'

'I didn't ask him. Just told him to think about it and get back to me when and if he made a decision.'

They chatted for a while, but when Jess had departed Phoebe felt worse than ever. She knew Charles wouldn't have considered such an ultimatum if she herself had delivered it, which proved his feelings for Jess were far stronger than they had ever been for her. So trying to make him jealous had been pointless.

And Nick David, knowing the situation, must have been aware of that futility!

So why had he done it? In the hope that she might influence her father's decision? It seemed to be the only answer.

The anger she'd felt earlier intensified, although now it was accompanied by an inner sadness she had no wish to analyse.

Time was the problem. Too much of it. Maybe she'd visit her mother. Spend the night and go somewhere for a picnic the following day.

Better than brooding all weekend.

She suited action to the thought, phoned her mother and packed a bag, including clothes to wear to work on Monday so she wouldn't have to return to the cottage. Tamborine markets would be on this Sunday. She and her mother could have a day up the mountain, and maybe dinner at Sanctuary Cove afterwards.

Keeping busy—that was the answer!

By Monday Phoebe had settled on a new plan. She would treat both her male colleagues at work as simply that—colleagues. She would be polite but remote, dedicated but reserved—totally professional.

'Where on earth have you been?' Nick loomed up behind her as she crossed the car park, causing problems with The New Plan before she'd even started on it. 'Obviously not at home or you'd have realised what had happened, even if you didn't get my note.'

'It's none of your business where I've been,' she told him, hoping she sounded more remote than she felt. 'And none of your business what

I do—which includes what I choose as a career.'

The memory of her father's revelations reminded her why 'remote' was good, and helped add a haughtiness to her voice.

Then the ambiguity of his final sentence struck her, and she stopped walking so she could turn to look at him. 'What note? What do you mean—I'd have realised what had happened? What's happened?'

The look of uncertainty on his face jabbed pain into her chest.

'Not Peter…' she faltered. 'He hasn't died?'

Sympathy made her abandon the remote scenario, and she grasped his arm to offer physical comfort.

But it seemed to make him more uncertain. Although he did cover her hand with his, and the reserved part of her New Plan suffered a severe setback.

'It's not Peter. He's as well as can be expected. It's you—well, not you. It was me. I was worried. You didn't answer the phone, or return my calls when I left a message on your machine. I couldn't stop thinking of the myriad forms of delayed reaction to head injury.'

He paused and Phoebe felt a sudden stillness in the morning air, as if the trees and birds and sunshine were all listening to his words.

'I contacted your father—he didn't have a key to your place, but with his parental authority and mine as a doctor, we got the police to break into your house.'

'You got the police to what?' Phoebe demanded, splitting the silence with her disbelieving shriek. 'And for your information, my father has had little parental authority over me since I was two when he left my mother for his second wife, so let's leave him out of this or any future conversations.'

'I was worried. I left you a note explaining what had happened—asking you to phone me,' Nick muttered lamely, glancing around at the other early arrivals whose walk across the car park had been arrested by Phoebe's furious reaction. 'Perhaps we should go inside. Continue this discussion there.'

She gave him a look that probably singed off his eyebrows, and stalked imperiously away. At least she was moving in the direction of the clinic. He hadn't lost her as a colleague.

Yet!

CHAPTER NINE

NICK followed more slowly, wondering how, in the short space of a week, his life could have gone from an orderly existence to such chaos. He'd always set goals for himself, and worked out priorities. Being a doctor had been an early ambition. The step to a skin cancer specialist had been a natural progression when Peter's melanoma had been diagnosed.

Since then, his life had been focussed on his work—on the three-pronged strategy he'd mapped out to take the clinic to the forefront of prevention, treatment and research of all forms of skin cancer.

Now a woman who, last Monday, had simply been part of the team working with him to achieve his goal was blurring his vision so the strategy was less important—his focus shot to pieces.

Not that he wouldn't get back on track, he promised himself. It had been concern for her health, nothing more, which had caused him such agonising apprehension over the weekend.

When he looked at it, it was the kiss that had started the problems. That first—and in retrospect disastrous—kiss. He'd kissed her out of kindness—and if he was totally honest with himself, because he'd always found her attractive and had been slightly piqued by her obvious preference for Charles.

But, for whatever reason, he'd done it, then damned if he hadn't been so affected by it he'd had to do it again.

And again.

Each one had been better than the last, promising more excitement, more enticement—addictive in a way he couldn't understand and didn't want to analyse.

Fortunately, if the way she'd stormed off earlier was any indication of how she felt about him, there'd be no more kisses—for any reason.

He plodded towards the hospital, wondering if he'd ever be able to regain the impetus that for so long had given purpose to his days and meaning to his life.

He flashed his ID at the guard and continued towards the rooms to check on the day's surgery patients. Smiled to himself. Phoebe had obviously forgotten she was scheduled to assist him today. How huffy could she stay when they'd be operating side by side?

Phoebe remembered the surgery as she walked into the clinic.

Perhaps Nick had forgotten he'd asked her.

She was trying to decide whether she'd be disappointed or relieved, should this be the case, when she heard his voice.

'We're due up in Theatre in twenty minutes, Phoebe,' he said, his voice carefully neutral.

Two could play the neutral game, she reminded herself, and she stowed her handbag in the filing cabinet and headed back out to the main area of the hospital. She'd need half those twenty minutes to change and scrub, then the rest of them checking on the instruments the theatre nurses would have set up.

Nick accompanied a drowsy Elizabeth Ramsey into the operating theatre.

'You'll be back in your hospital bed before you know it,' he assured her.

He nodded to Phoebe to acknowledge her presence, and she managed to nod back, pleased she wasn't expected to speak as her mouth had gone dry.

Though why it should have when all she could see of the man was the gap between his mask and the concealing surgical cap—a gap that contained two cool blue-green eyes—she didn't know.

'Do you know why we're doing this operation?' Nick asked, directing the question to one of the three students who'd followed him into theatre.

'To remove a small basal cell carcinoma from the patient's leg,' one of them, a young woman, replied.

'Doctors remove BCCs from patients every day of the week,' Nick reminded her. 'Why in Theatre under a general anaesthetic?'

'Because you'll need a skin graft?' the student guessed, and Phoebe imagined she could hear Nick's teeth grind.

'Keep talking—why might she need that?' he persisted, and when the student shrugged he continued, 'Why you lot don't read the patient's history before you come into Theatre I'll never know.'

He turned to Phoebe.

'Would you like to explain to these young hopefuls?' he growled, passing responsibility to her and turning to check the instruments laid out on the trolley.

'Mrs Ramsey has a history of skin cancer and has had perhaps as many as a hundred lesions removed from her legs, arms and face. This one is between old, scarred skin so it's possible it's a continuation of a BCC which has already been removed. The problem is that small patches of malignant cells can stream between the collagen bundles and lurk beneath skin which appears quite normal.'

'But don't doctors have guidelines for the removal of all suspect lesions?' one of the students asked. 'I mean, don't they have to excise a particular margin around the lesion and have that tested to make sure they got the lot?'

'Theoretically, yes,' Phoebe told him, 'but although that was undoubtedly done when the original lesion was removed from Mrs Ramsey's leg, it's possible the margins were clear but there was cancerous involvement beyond them.'

'Which is why we're using Mohs' technique this time,' Nick explained. 'The stain we use will show up any further migration of the cancer cells, and we can remove the lot. We do, of course, use it in day surgery situations and even in the skin-cancer clinic itself, taking thin layers of tissue and testing each one. In this case, however, the site and the extent of previous damage to the surrounding skin indicates we will probably need to graft new skin over the wound, and there's the possibility the wound could be extensive.'

He waved Phoebe into place beside him as the theatre sister pulled the plastic-wrapped microscope into position for them.

Using the eyepiece meant close body contact, something Phoebe could have lived without. She tried desperately to concentrate on the job at hand and regain her usual detachment from the physical closeness of surgery.

But her body would have none of it—reacting to Nick's with tremors and heat and pathetic longings which her mind was powerless to control. The colours of the dye swirled outward, Nick's scalpel following, selecting carefully, excising. It was her job to spread layers of excised skin onto slides, then pass them to the nurse who'd transfer them to the pathologist on duty for immediate consideration. But in her head the colours of attraction swirled as vividly, confusing and weakening her.

'Have you used a dermatome before?' Nick asked, and she realised, belatedly, he was talking to her.

'To harvest skin for a graft?' she muttered, as she dredged the name of the electric knife used for this operation out of her befuddled brain.

'What else?'

The question was short, and sharp. Fair enough, given her apparent vagueness. She did the pulling-herself-together thing again and rallied.

'Yes,' she told him. Then, because she could feel a tension in the room, beyond what was happening in her body, she added, 'Piece of cake.'

'Good. Then you can do the harvest.'

Before she could protest, the nurse was handing her the instrument and pointing to the already prepped patch of thigh left uncovered by the surgical drapes.

Phoebe felt her fingers tremble on the instrument. Nick had asked her to assist last week. Back when he'd been plotting with her father to have her specialise.

Which was probably why he'd made the offer.

These thoughts, which had nothing to do with the task before her, raced through her head, then she straightened, determined to show him just how good a specialist she would have been.

Had she cared to follow that path!

She set the rotary blade in motion and carefully removed a slice of skin less than a millimetre thick. The nurse lifted it and passed it to Nick who placed it carefully across the wound. While he stitched it into place, Phoebe covered the donor site with a sterile, non-adhesive dressing. The wound was weeping and would continue to do so for a few days. In fact, in some cases, it could take longer to heal than the site which had the graft.

'So, what did you learn?' Nick asked the students, when Elizabeth Ramsey had been wheeled into Recovery and they were stripping off their outer gowns, replacing them with clean ones.

'Harvesting skin is a piece of cake?' the cheeky young man suggested, sending a smile in Phoebe's direction.

Nick cooled whatever pleasure that might have given her by directing a stern frown her way.

'Apart from my assistant's flippancy!' he muttered.

'Cancerous cells from a BCC can migrate and not be found, except by the use of this surgery?'

It was the young woman who answered, and she won a smile from Nick.

'Exactly!' he said.

'But does that mean all BCCs should be excised this way?' the third student asked.

Nick shook his head.

'Simple excision of the lesion and the margins is usually enough, but if you suspect the tumour is an extension of an older one, then Mohs' is the way to go. If it's migrated once, chances are it will do it again, so go for the lot. It's ninety-eight per cent effective.'

Which your immunity used to be, Phoebe thought as she stood aside and studied Nick as he chatted to the group. Had it only been The Kiss which had destroyed it? Or had, dread thought, the attraction been there all along, and she'd forced herself towards a preference for Charles as a measure of self-preservation?

Thoroughly confused, she turned away, intending to change as Nick hadn't asked her to assist with any other operation.

'Not staying to watch my expertise for the rest of the morning?'

His voice made her turn, and what she imagined was a different question in his eyes made her shake her head.

She remembered how angry she was with him and rallied.

'The young man we met at the beach might have turned up. Even if I've missed him, I'd like to know what Charles has told him—what he's decided to do.'

Nick nodded.

'Let me know later,' he said, so absent-mindedly she guessed his mind had returned to the day's surgical procedures.

So much for questioning eyes!

She walked away, more confused than ever.

Nick knew she'd gone, although he was speaking to the students again, explaining about the lentigo maligna he was about to remove from the next patient's left cheek.

'It's a slow-growing malignancy which we often monitor for change before surgery,' he explained, while thinking himself of the not-so-slow growing attraction he felt for Phoebe and what he could possibly do about it. 'When we do decide to operate we use a special light which shows up the extent of the tumour in much the same way as the dye we use for Mohs' gives us the boundaries of the BCC involvement.'

And special light—like that of Phoebe's namesake, the moon—hadn't shown up much more than the strength of his attraction—or was it the depths of his weakness?

He had to stop kissing her for a start.

Not that she'd be likely to let him that close again. What had possessed him to—?

'Skin graft?'

He had to guess at the question as he hauled his mind back to work-related topics.

'Usually we can simply draw the edges of the wound together, although if the excision is wide we do use grafts.'

He went on to explain the appearance of the tan freckle that was typical of lentigo maligna, which could thicken and develop into a malignancy if left untreated.

Untreated! Would his attraction to Phoebe develop a malignancy if left untreated? And how the hell could he treat it anyway?

Taking her to bed was the obvious answer. Experience had told him it was the allure of the unknown that heightened sexual attraction.

Taking the object of desire to bed was like scratching an itch.

He grinned to himself as he imagined Phoebe's fiery reaction to that philosophy, and amended the scratching metaphor to excising a skin lesion.

Not that it would ever happen.

Back to work, Nick David, and put Phoebe Moreton right out of your head!

Which wasn't any easier to do than banishing the effect of her from his body. He made this gloomy discovery as he sat in Peter's room later in the day, eating the slightly stale sandwich Peter had left on his tray.

'It's not exactly encouraging for a patient when his doctor sits beside his bed and sighs so heavily,' Peter told him.

Nick, dismayed to find he'd been behaving so badly, rallied, smiling at his friend and apologising for his preoccupation.

'Don't apologise,' Peter said. 'You've no idea what a relief it is to have you preoccupied with something other than me.' He smiled quizzically at Nick and added, 'I assume it isn't me causing you so much mental anguish?'

'It should be,' Nick told him. 'I don't know what's happening. Normally, at this stage of your treatment, I'm totally focussed on what's going on inside your body.'

'Exactly what I've been trying to tell you for years, old mate. You've been too damn focussed! You've got to get a life!'

Nick began to protest, but Peter held up his frail hand.

'No, let me finish! I know you've pretended to have a life—even going so far as to parade a line of lovely women past me in an attempt to convince me—but I know, and deep down you know, that you put your life on hold from the day I was diagnosed. Almost as if you felt if I couldn't have a long and happy future, you didn't deserve one either.'

'That's nonsense,' Nick told him. 'It's not as if you haven't had a lot of good years since then. Boy! You more than rivalled me in the parade-of-lovely-women stakes. Remember Bette Sinclair?'

Peter smiled, then shook his head.

'You're not going to divert me from this conversation with images of wild young women, Nick. I'm serious. We had a lot of fun together—but I had reason to be living in the present, without thought for a future I couldn't always face. You, on the other hand, are getting too old for the love 'em and leave 'em game. It's time to think ahead—to settle down.'

Nick studied him, wondering whether they were so closely attuned to each other that Peter had read some of his troubled thoughts.

He wanted to reject Peter's words, to say, I've plenty of time. But that would have been too cruel a reminder of Peter's lack of time— for both of them.

'Why this sudden burst of philosophy?' he asked instead. 'Has Mum been visiting you?'

Peter smiled and shook his head.

'Maybe I feel it's time for both of us to move on. I've enjoyed the vicarious experience of your mating-dating game, so what about the next stage? What about letting me in on a little secondhand insight into the real stuff? I know you've got all these hang-ups about marriage because of your mum, but surely you're old enough now to get over that. Old enough to try the "courtship, marriage, child" idea. How good's your predicting ability? Your prognosticating? Have I got time for you to have a baby? A godchild for me? Perhaps a Peter or a Petra?'

Nick swallowed the huge lump which had grown in his throat—presumably as the result of eating a stale sandwich.

He peered at his friend and decided flippancy was the only way to respond. 'Gee whiz, mate, you're not asking much! There's only a nine months' lead time for the baby thing, and you've got heaps of time for that, but courting? Holy cow! I could be twelve months just getting over the shock, then another twelve learning the moves.'

He leaned forward, pretending to give it serious consideration, while his stomach churned with panic.

'Then a twelve month engagement during which time whoever I've found would probably discover enough about me to run a mile, and I'd have to start over again. Can you hang around for another five years? Maybe ten? Damn! I'll have to put some heat under that research department. We've got to come up with something better in the way of treatment—and fast. Maybe if we can cure you, you can do the baby thing yourself. Save me the hassle.'

Peter chuckled at his performance, but Nick knew his friend would read it as just that—a show. If Peter had another two years, they'd both be lucky.

'So you'll have to fast-track the programme, won't you?' Peter said, seemingly attuned to Nick's mind again. 'I mean with the courtship scenario, not the research.'

He lay back against his pillows, a signal he was tired and needed to sleep.

Nick touched his hand and left the room, his mind now churning as rebelliously as his stomach.

Marriage...

With regular work finished for the day, Phoebe sat at her desk, hunched over Phil's patient file. The lad had come, as directed, to the clinic and Charles had fitted him in before their regular patients.

And had booked him for surgery tomorrow.

She thought of the young man she'd met on the beach and felt a wave of sympathy wash through her. The urgency of the surgery told her all she needed to know—except why Charles had chosen to admit Phil to hospital for the surgery rather than do it in Day Surgery.

'Is that Phil's file?'

Nick's voice made her turn and she saw that he and Charles had both walked into the room.

Phoebe nodded and handed him the slim folder, then, more to divert her mind and body from lustful thoughts than anything else, she asked Charles the question which had been puzzling her.

'We're going to try to identify the sentinel node—the lymph node that's the main one draining the tumour site,' he explained.

Phoebe felt a lurch of excitement.

'I've read some of the papers coming out of America about this technique,' she said, smiling warmly at Charles. Possibly too warmly if Nick's frown was anything to go on. 'In fact, about all the exciting options nuclear medicine is offering to cancer patients. It might sound fearsome, the word ''nuclear'', but fancy being able to use radioactive material to target just the bad cells of a tumour, rather than destroying surrounding tissue and good cells. Who's doing it? You?'

Charles nodded and crossed the room, dragging Sheree's office chair with him and sitting down next to Phoebe.

'I was tempted to excise it and take all the lymph nodes as well, but the kid's so young that if we can track the disease this way, he'll have far less pain and scarring.'

Nick joined the conversation, reminding Charles that if the first node proved positive they'd have to take the lot anyway, but Charles had seen the boy and was confident the melanoma hadn't spread.

'You inject a special substance around the site, is that right?' Phoebe said, hoping to divert an argument which seemed to be building.

'Yes—or around the biopsy scar if it's already been excised,' Charles told her. 'Better by far to do it before operating on the malignancy. Once the dye's injected, the patient is transferred to the nuclear medicine suite where a gamma camera and a hand-held gamma probe will show up a ''hot spot'' where the injected material gathers. This is our sentinel node, and all we have to do is mark the spot then, in Theatre, make a small incision and, again checking with a gamma probe, remove the single lymph node.'

'We'll also remove the melanoma,' Nick said dryly.

Something in his tone made Phoebe turn towards him, and she met eyes that were studying her with a perplexed look she'd never seen before.

Probably wondering if she was still angry with him, which she was when she remembered the revelations of the weekend—not to mention breaking into her house.

Though she was partly to blame for all her problems, she admitted to herself when Charles stood up and moved away, asking Nick a question and diverting the man's attention from her.

Nick might have had his own reasons for seeking her out and initiating the charade, but at least he had been playing for slightly higher and definitely more noble stakes as he'd had the financial stability of the clinic in mind.

For her, there was no excuse. She should never have stooped to such a pathetic and immature ruse as attempting to make Charles jealous.

And definitely not continued with it after experiencing The Kiss.

She was still musing on all of this when the sound of the office door closing made her look up. It must have been Charles who'd departed, for Nick remained, standing in the middle of the room and looking down at her with a slightly startled expression on his face.

'I don't suppose you'd like to marry me?' he said, which, she guessed, left both of them looking startled.

'Soon?' he added, although his gloomy tone suggested he expected a negative reply.

Or that the idea had all the appeal of eating bad seafood.

'You're obviously mad!' Phoebe told him, when she'd gathered enough brain cells back together to string words into a sentence. 'First you plot with my father about my career, then you break into my house, and now you're asking me to marry you? I don't even *like* you, Nick David.'

'I didn't think you would,' he muttered.

She was watching him as she spoke and had to admit, if only to herself, that he did the woebegone look quite well. If she hadn't known better, she'd have been almost tempted to believe he was disappointed.

But she did know better, so she leaned forward and dragged her handbag out of the filing cabinet, then stood up, tilted her chin and strode across the room, determined to put as much space between herself and this man as she possibly could.

Unfortunately it wasn't much, for he caught her arm as she whisked past, effectively stopping her regal progress.

'You can't go home,' he said, almost stuttering over the words in his haste to get them said. 'Well, not alone. Not without me.'

Phoebe gave him what she hoped was an icy glare, then shook his hand off her arm.

'If you think you're coming home with me, you've got another think coming, buster!' she fumed, forgetting momentarily she was speaking to her boss. 'It's bad enough I'm contracted to *work* with you for another six months, without having you intruding into my private life. Marry you indeed!'

She stormed away, but didn't get far.

'Phoebe,' he said, as he caught hold of her yet again, 'I'll admit the marriage thing was a mistake. I'd been brooding over something Peter said and it just popped out. Now, come down off your high horse for just one minute and listen to me.' He turned her so he was looking down into her face. 'I know I'm not making much sense. Believe me, it's not making much sense to me either but, all that aside, there's a physical reason you can't go home. Well, not without a key. When we broke in, the lock was ruined. I changed it, of course. It was the least I could do. But you need a new key. That's why I left you a note.'

She heard the words but their meaning wasn't all that clear because her mind was busy telling her body it didn't want to lean towards Nick's and telling her lips there was no way she was going to kiss him. She was far, far too angry with him.

He was speaking again, something about the key being at his apartment. She raised her eyes from alluring lips to questing eyes, and felt her heart falter at the intensity of his gaze.

He was talking about her front door key, for heaven's sake. Seduction was the furthest thing from his mind. Even that ridiculous proposal had been generated, for some reason, by his visit to his friend.

She must have nodded as she scolded herself, or in some way indicated agreement to something, for now he'd taken her arm and was ushering her out of the office—out of the clinic.

Should she pretend she knew exactly where they were going, or should she ask?

Given her current state of total confusion, asking was definitely the only way out.

'Where are we going?'

He stopped abruptly, frowning fiercely, then his expression softened as he looked into her face and his fingers gently touched her temple where the slight wound from the accident had scabbed over.

'Are you sure you're all right? No headache? Blurred vision?'

Standing so close, her body began thinking kisses once again—and her mouth felt dry with anticipation. She shook her head to answer his question, wondering if men felt the same plucking at their nerves she was experiencing at that moment.

If this man felt it...

'Then are you listening this time?' he asked sternly, and she nodded.

'I left the key to your new lock at home. I suggested you might like to come home with me for dinner as it's the least I can do by way of apology after causing that fuss yesterday, then I'll drop you back here at your car when I come in to visit Peter later.'

This time Phoebe heard the words—and was amazed.

'You said all of that?' she demanded.

'More, in fact—that was just a summary,' Nick said, a wry grin moving the distracting lips. 'I must be prattling on too much during our work time together if you can tune out so successfully.'

'No! No! Not at all!' Phoebe protested. 'I was thinking of something else, that's all.'

She crossed her fingers behind her back—hoping for sufficient luck to stop him asking what had occupied her mind.

'So what's the answer? You did nod, which seemed like agreement, but as you didn't know the question…'

If she hadn't known him better, she'd have thought he sounded uncertain. Although it might have been embarrassment. If she'd organised for the police to break down someone's door, she'd be embarrassed.

'It isn't rocket science, Phoebe!' he muttered, more irritated than uncertain now. 'Not something that needs great mental effort. Do you want a bite to eat at my place or not? That's all you have to decide.'

'Not,' she told him. Put like that, the decision was easy. She'd have opted out of any similar danger—like running across a street in front of a bus, or leaping into the lion's cage at the zoo. 'I'll follow you home to collect the key. You don't owe me anything for breaking in. In fact, I should be grateful to you for your concern.'

Nick bit back the growl of frustration that tried to issue forth from his lips and strode towards the car park. Damn the woman! Let her keep up if she could. She was tying him in knots. It was Peter's fault. Mentioning this marriage thing.

Suddenly, relieving his physical attraction by getting Phoebe into bed had seemed possible—not a love 'em and leave 'em scenario after all. He could marry her, and kill two birds with one stone.

Then he'd stupidly blurted out a lacklustre proposal the first moment he'd been alone with her and had brought well-deserved scorn down on his head.

He shook his head, and turned to see her climbing in behind the wheel of her own car.

Should he try again when she followed him home? Perhaps suggest dinner somewhere else?

'No, thank you,' she said calmly, when he mooted this idea. She was standing on the pavement outside his apartment block, her car parked in the loading zone but with the engine running in case he didn't get the message that her presence was only temporary. 'If you could just get the key I'll be on my way.'

He wanted to explain, to tell her about Peter's request tilting his world sideways, but something told him he'd only make things worse.

'I'll get the key,' he agreed, and walked away.

CHAPTER TEN

AFTER the cool, calm and collected approach had worked so well for Phoebe on Monday evening, she decided to stick with it at work. Greeting Nick with politeness but keeping a good dose of reserve between them. Phil's surgery on the Tuesday went well, with no sign of the malignancy showing up in the sentinel lymph node.

The good news gave everyone in the unit a special zest so the working days passed swiftly and a sense of optimism permeated the air. Jess was confident she could put together a programme for Mr Abrams, approval had come through for treating Jackie with the new protocols and even Peter seemed a little better, his stubborn tumours slowly responding to his body's newly triggered defence mechanisms.

'What are you wearing to the ball?' Jess asked, when she and Phoebe met up in the canteen at lunchtime on Thursday.

'I'm not going,' Phoebe told her, and hid the ache that saying the words out loud had caused.

'Of course you are,' Jess said sternly. 'Nick was talking about our table and counted you in, and Charles has been complaining for a week about you dumping him out of your car just so you could buy a new dress.'

'I thought you weren't seeing Charles,' Phoebe said, hoping to divert Jess from the ball topic.

Jess smiled dreamily.

'We've worked it out,' she said, then added, 'Boy! Have we ever worked it out!'

The words were so heavily laden with sexual undertones that Phoebe felt embarrassed, but a dull ache in her body suggested envy was involved as well.

Jess, eyes sparkling with love, began to talk about the resumption of her relationship with Charles, and as she prattled happily on, Phoebe's ache became a sharper pain. Added to the sense of loss and loneliness she'd been experiencing lately, it made her a less than ideal companion, but Jess didn't appear to notice.

Although some of Phoebe's side of the conversation must have stayed with Jess, a fact which became obvious much later that afternoon.

'What's this nonsense Jess tells me about you not coming to the ball?' Nick demanded.

They were up on the ward, Phoebe coming out of Jackie Stubbings's room and Nick emerging from Peter's.

'You only asked me because of the Charles business, and as it's now patently obvious even to an idiot like me that he never had much interest in me in the first place, there's no point.'

'But you've bought a dress,' Nick reminded her, and Phoebe wondered just how much tooth enamel she would lose if she gave in to a desire to grind them. Hard!

'I buy dresses quite often!' she informed Nick, her lofty tones in keeping with The New Plan. 'I really don't see why the occasion should be of such interest to half the staff of this hospital.'

He seemed disconcerted, which was good, but soon rallied—which was bad.

'Listen, Phoebe,' he began, 'aren't you being just a little pig-headed about this? It's a once-a-year social occasion which staff from all over the hospital attend—many of them simply as friends and colleagues. Drive yourself, if you like, or get a cab. I can understand if you don't want people thinking we're together but, on the other hand, I wouldn't want anyone thinking there's disharmony in the unit. You'll come? Please?'

Phoebe studied him. He sounded genuine enough. The clinic boss wanting all his staff together. One big happy family. Showing the flag and nothing more!

This realisation caused such pain she had to bite back a whimper of disappointment. Ridiculous to think he'd want you there for his sake, she told herself.

And if you don't go after he's put it that way, you'll seem petty.

'I suppose I'll come,' she grouched, and Nick frowned at her.

'Well, don't force yourself,' he snapped, and stalked off, running slap-bang into the trolley pushed by a woman who was collecting the patients' dinner dishes.

The noise was unbelievable as plates, cutlery and aluminium plate-covers crashed and clattered to the ground.

Phoebe darted forward, extricating the woman first, checking that she was uninjured, hearing Nick's curses as he wiped broccoli from the lapels of his suit. Nurses and orderlies appeared from all directions.

'Come on!' Nick said to her, snatching broken pieces of crockery from her hands and setting them down on the trolley. 'There are enough people cleaning up. Let's get out of here before you cause any more problems.'

'M-me cause problems?' Phoebe stammered, grabbing a paper towel to wipe debris from her fingers as she followed him out of the ward into the corridor. 'I didn't run into that woman!'

'No, but you caused it all the same,' Nick said darkly, then he pushed open a door and stepped through it.

The unfair accusation gave Phoebe enough cause to vent the anger which had simmered for days. Seeing her quarry about to disappear, she followed him, then backed out, burning red with embarrassment, after one brief glimpse of gleaming stainless-steel urinals.

'Giving up so easily, Phoebe?'

Nick's mocking words followed her out and haunted her as she headed home. Although it was the spin she put on them which most affected her—because it reminded her she *had* given up. On The Plan! The old plan, not the new one.

Which meant her one great chance of finally getting rid of her virginity was now lost.

The sense of loss which swept through her was so acute she wondered if it could possibly be something else. A physical malady.

Like her loss of appetite.

By Saturday she was so uptight she wondered if she could plead illness to avoid the ball. Her stomach was certainly upset, and her entire body ached with tension. She'd promised Jackie she'd call at the hospital to show her The Dress, but did she really have to go on to the convention centre, where the ball was being held?

'Fancy meeting you here. Did you drive or would you like a lift to the convention centre?'

Nick's voice slid into her ears as she stood just inside Peter's room and blushed at their patient's praise for her appearance. Her heart sank as she realised her boss's arrival had put paid to any idea of escaping the main event.

She turned slowly, wondering how on earth she'd come to pay money for a garment that covered so little of her body and showed so much bare skin. Particularly bare skin that was reacting to the sight of Nick in a dinner suit with unseemly warmth and tiny prickles of excitement.

'I...'

The words dried on her lips as she raised her head to answer him and saw the expression in his eyes. More a glow than an expression, something fierce and primeval that raised goose-bumps on her arms.

Great—now I've got goose-bumps as well as prickles and pinkness, she thought irrelevantly while she struggled to control her breathing and get words out of her mouth.

'Well, if Peter's had enough looks, we'll go, shall we?' Nick took her silence for agreement and grasped her arm with a brusqueness that startled her.

It may also have startled him for he dropped it almost as quickly as he'd touched it, and somehow herded her from the room, not in physical contact but definitely getting across the message that she should move.

The sleek Mercedes she'd followed home during the week was parked in the specialists' area right outside the door and, still too bemused—and confused—to protest, Phoebe allowed herself to be led towards it.

'I suppose you can sit down in that dress?' Nick said, and, fearing sarcasm, Phoebe's head snapped up. Once again she was spoiling for a fight!

But Nick was smiling, and the teasing gleam in his eyes undid her anger and further weakened her resistance to the man.

'Just!' she told him and slid into the soft leather seat.

Nick held the strap of the seat belt out to her. 'Belt up,' he said, and the smile appeared again. 'I'd offer to do it for you but I'm not sure I'd be able to answer for the consequences of leaning across you.'

He shut the door before she could question the remark, but as he walked around the front of the car, then seated himself beside her, the warm glow she felt suggested it must have been a compliment.

Not that he showed her any further attention, discussing Peter's progress on the short drive to the convention centre, then leading her into the ballroom without laying a finger on any part of her body.

Detached didn't begin to describe his behaviour.

Phoebe fought a sense of pique as she followed him, then a little uncertainty that The Dress wasn't quite as great as she'd hoped. But when Sheree's husband whistled, and Charles looked startled—well, more like stunned—she decided it must be OK and accepted a glass of champagne from a passing waiter.

'Fantastic!' Jess whispered to her, when Phoebe sat down beside her. 'You'll knock his socks off!'

'Whose socks?' Phoebe asked, remembering rather guiltily that Charles's socks had been the target.

'Nick's, of course,' Jess told her. 'And don't bother telling me you're not interested. The electricity the pair of you generate could light the entire hospital.'

'Well, I'm *not* interested,' Phoebe said stoutly, although the rapid patter of her heartbeats made a nonsense of her denial.

Fortunately, appetisers arrived at that moment, and talk turned to which one to choose. Nick, who'd been standing behind Phoebe and discussing radiotherapy with a hospital colleague, passed the plate to her, but her appetite, after deserting her the previous week, had failed to return, and she eyed all the attractive offerings with distaste.

'You must be sickening for something if you're not eating,' Charles said, with the hearty joviality of a man determined to enjoy the evening.

Then Jess made things worse by murmuring, 'Love?' under her breath.

The thought that it could possibly be anything other than lust she felt for Nick was startling, to say the least. Phoebe found herself musing over it while conversations swirled around her. As they were attached to the oncology ward's table, there were plenty of people milling around. Between picking at food she didn't want, she danced, and talked, and must have been making the right noises for no one questioned her detachment.

But the puzzle over love, in all its guises, remained the focus of her mind. The words batted back and forth by fellow party-goers became nothing more than background noise, and she barely realised that Jess had shifted from beside her and Charles had taken her place.

Until she heard his voice.

'That's hardly the kind of dress I'd expect to see you wearing to an occasion like this,' he said, his disapproval etching like acid into her skin.

Phoebe felt tears prickle behind her eyelids and knew they were more the result of her own confusion than Charles's mean-spirited comment, but she had to sniff them away and was still wondering how to answer when a warm hand gripped her shoulder.

'My dance, I think,' Nick said, sliding his hand to her upper arm and all but hoisting her out of the chair.

She stumbled to her feet and felt him steady her, then take her gently in his arms and whirl her out onto the dance floor.

Battling humiliation now as well as the effects of his closeness on her body, she gave herself up to the music and let Nick lead her in the dance.

The music slowed and he drew her closer, tucking her against his body and holding her as if she were fragile—and perhaps precious.

'It's a lovely dress,' he murmured into her ear. 'A classy dress. A delectable, delicious, delightful dress. My only problem with it is I keep imagining myself taking it off. It's that kind of dress, sweet Phoebe, so don't let that curmudgeonly Charles tell you otherwise.'

Phoebe heard the words and snuggled closer. Her body was already in transports of delight and now her mind was suggesting Nick had given her the very opening she needed.

Dimly she tried to recall how many glasses of champagne she'd had in case the bubbly might be the cause of the brainwave, but she was reasonably certain it had only been two, so the brilliance of the idea wasn't alcohol induced. Though the courage to speak might have had a little alcoholic backing.

'You could take it off,' she whispered back, studying his ear lobe so she didn't have to meet his eyes. 'Not now, but later. If you liked.'

For someone who'd had a plan, it didn't sound too convincing, but as Nick's body grew tense and he missed the beat, trod on her foot and then thrust her suddenly away from him, she guessed convincing didn't matter.

Somehow, she'd got the message across.

'*What* did you say?' Nick demanded, finding his feet but needing all his restraint to keep his voice below a bellow. He glared at the woman who'd turned from biddable colleague into… Well, he didn't know what she'd turned into but whatever it was, it was disrupting his well-ordered life.

Colour had risen in her cheeks and her eyes sparkled with challenge as they gamely met his.

'Do you really want me to repeat it? Say it louder maybe?'

He shook his head and groaned, then realised people were looking at them and shuffled back into some kind of rhythm.

'What do you mean, I can take it off later?' he asked again, only more quietly this time, directing the words to where her ear was hidden by a thickness of shiny dark hair.

'Just that,' she said with a new meekness that made him extremely suspicious. 'Back at your place. Or at my place. I don't know much about seduction scenes, or how they're supposed to be played—lack of experience, you see—but I thought you might like to know I wouldn't mind. In fact, I'd be grateful. Very grateful. It's embarrassing, being a virgin at my age.'

He was just coming to terms with what Phoebe had suggested when the second flood of words illuminated everything for him.

It also convinced him that no amount of restraint would keep his voice below bellowing
level. He steered his partner towards the win-
dows, danced her across the wide patio, then
led her forcibly down the steps to where he
was reasonably certain no one would hear him.

'You want me to take you home to bed in
order to help you over some hang-up you've
got about not having had sex with anyone? Is
that what this is all about?' he growled. 'What
do you think I am? Some kind of stud who
goes around relieving women of their virginity—'

'I think stud-muffin's the latest word,'
Phoebe put in helpfully. She was now fairly
certain it must have been three glasses of
champagne, and was a little afraid of what to
do next.

'Don't interrupt,' Nick roared at her, but he
seemed to have lost his train of thought because he hesitated, giving her the opportunity
to speak again.

'I'm sorry. It was a silly idea. But Jess said
you had experience, and our kisses were OK—
I mean, I really liked them—and we're both
adults with no ties to anyone else, so I
thought... But obviously I was wrong. I'd bet-

ter go back in. We should really both go back in. We don't want people talking.'

'No, we don't,' Nick said, but the words sounded strangled and she felt a moment's pity for him. No doubt he was even more confused than she was.

She walked away, hoping the night air would cool the burning heat of embarrassment she could feel in her cheeks. As she re-entered the ballroom, a young intern whom she'd met on the oncology ward greeted her with delight and begged for a dance.

Going home to bed, pulling the covers over her head and staying there for a year or two would have been her first choice of what to do next, but the young man was pleading and as she couldn't leave immediately after her precipitate departure to the gardens with Nick, without causing some comment, she agreed.

She had danced maybe six steps with the intern when a familiar figure loomed up behind him, tapped him on the shoulder and said, in a voice that brooked no argument, 'I'm cutting in.' Without waiting for a reply, Nick detached Phoebe from the intern's arms and settled her in his own.

'That was extremely rude!' she snarled at him.

'Tough!' he said, moving his body in some way that drew her closer.

'You don't have to dance with me. You can't possibly want to,' she muttered, while her body argued that dancing with Nick was exactly what *it* wanted.

Well, not exactly perhaps, but coming close.

'I'll decide what I want and don't want,' he replied. 'And right now I've decided to dance with you. Besides, I'm your boss, and to a certain extent responsible for your welfare. Who knows what other poor fool you might proposition tonight if I leave you on your own?'

Heat burned in Phoebe's cheeks again, and she dipped her head, hoping her hair would hide the vivid evidence of her embarrassment. Her feet, which should have been stumbling in confusion, seemed to follow his by instinct, so once again she gave in to the music and to the pretence that she was in Nick's arms because that's where he wanted her to be.

Big mistake!

Her body seemed to think it was OK to lean closer to him, and to respond to his presence with all the fluttery excitement his kisses had induced. The ache deep in her belly begged to be eased, and her nipples peaked and prickled with a painful desire.

But although Nick's body moulded itself to hers, and although she imagined that physical reactions so strong couldn't be all one-sided, nothing he said or did betrayed the slightest weakness in his very attractive flesh.

In the end, it all became too much. When the band finally stopped for a break, Phoebe waited until they'd returned to the table then, while Jess was teasing Nick about only dancing with one woman, she excused herself and slipped away, making it as far as the corridor outside the ballroom before Nick caught up with her.

'Leaving early, Cinderella?' he asked, his eyes glittering strangely as he looked down into her face.

'She left at midnight. I've stayed an extra hour,' Phoebe told him, trying to speak calmly although she was jittery with both the excitement his presence caused and the humiliation of her memories.

'I'll drive you home, unless you've a convenient pumpkin you can summon up.'

He sounded as calm as she was pretending to be, but the strange light remained in his eyes.

'It's OK,' she said, with a casual shrug of her shoulder to add to her pretence of control. 'Cabs or pumpkins, it's all the same to me. I know after the way I behaved earlier the last thing you'd want to do is drive me home. I'm sorry if I embarrassed or offended you.'

She wanted to mention the champagne but couldn't bring herself to use it as an excuse when, in fact, she'd actually conceived the foolish plan while stone-cold sober.

'I'll still drive you home,' he said, and took her arm, his touch reminding her of all the reasons she didn't want to be alone with him.

Or near him. Cooped up in a car. Smelling his cologne, his maleness.

Dancing had been bad enough, but at least in front of several hundred people she'd been forced to practise what little decorum she'd managed to retain.

'I'd rather get a cab,' she muttered, trying to draw away.

'I think you've forfeited your choice,' he said, and Phoebe shivered at the strangeness in his eyes. 'After all, I can hardly take the dress off here, can I?'

Nick felt the shudder that ripped through her body, and felt her arm tremble in his hand.

He cursed himself for letting the rage of his confusion loose, but couldn't unsay the words.

Couldn't speak at all when she turned and looked at him.

'Haven't you punished me enough?' she asked, her voice husky with the tears he could see shimmering in her eyes. 'Making me dance with you like that? All the time looking so grim no one could suppose you were enjoying it. I did a foolish thing, Nick. But, hell, aren't we both adults? Aren't women supposed to be allowed to say such things these days? My mistake was in thinking you might not see it as a chore. That you might actually enjoy it.'

He saw her throat move convulsively, then she added, in a very small voice, 'That we might both actually enjoy it.'

Nick's fingers had slackened their hold on her arm and she moved away, her head bowed, the dark glossy tresses swinging forward to hide a face he guessed was streaked by tears.

A weight like a grand piano lodged in his chest and he followed, staying behind her, not wanting to add to the humiliation she was obviously feeling. As a cab slid to a stop in front of her forlorn figure, he stepped forward and opened the door for her, then leaned in to tell the cabbie her address, passing him a note and adjuring him to take care of her.

Then, because he found he couldn't bear to see her so unhappy, he touched her gently on the cheek.

'It'll be OK,' he said. 'We'll both get past this and turn up to work again on Monday as if nothing's happened.'

But as the taxi drove away he wasn't so certain. He couldn't imagine how much courage it must have taken for a young woman as reserved as Phoebe to have made such a suggestion, or what damage he'd done to her ego with his vitriolic rebuff.

Although there was one thing he did know for damn sure—it would be a long time before his body forgave him for not taking her up on the offer.

CHAPTER ELEVEN

WHEN the world failed to implode or otherwise destroy itself by Monday, Phoebe dragged herself reluctantly out of bed, glared at a sun that shone too brightly through her window and studied the contents of her wardrobe with gloomy dissatisfaction.

What the hell did one wear when facing one's boss after he'd turned down a sexual proposition? It was worse than last Monday morning, when all she'd done had been to slam her door in his face.

No early training in manners or decorum had ever covered this situation.

Cover—that was a clue. The more covered she was, the less hotly flushed skin would be on show. She pulled out a suit in the fine natural-coloured linen she favoured for work. Trousers, although she usually wore a skirt, a simple knitted vest top and a long sleeved jacket. That should do the trick.

Talking to herself by way of encouragement, she showered, dressed and left the house, arriving at work early to avoid meeting other staff in the car park.

'Good morning, Phoebe.'

The bumps had already risen on her arms so she hadn't needed the voice to confirm that the footsteps catching up to her were Nick's.

'Good morning, Nick,' she managed, remembering his parting words on Saturday night.

'We're taking cells from one of Jackie's tumours today—before her next lot of chemo starts. I won't be in the unit much but you and Charles will manage.'

So he'd meant what he'd said, Phoebe realised, although this pretence that nothing had happened was obviously coming easier to him than it was to her.

She mumbled something about carrying on regardless but was distracted by the inexplicable regret lodged in her heart.

Surely she couldn't be sorry nothing had happened? Think of the consequences if it had!

She shuddered, then felt Nick touch her arm.

'OK?' he asked, his voice gentle with concern.

She looked up at him, met his eyes but couldn't read their expression, although the blue-green depths left her more breathless than usual.

'I'm OK,' she said stoutly, but knew it was a lie. She might never be OK again.

Not if it was love.

'Hi, you two. You coming to work or not? Did you enjoy the ball, Phoebe? Fantastic dress. You had Gerry's eyeballs out on stalks. I told him I'd have to belt him one if he kept drooling over you.'

Sheree overtook them, and her description of her husband's reaction made Phoebe smile. Everyone who knew Sheree and Gerry knew he worshipped the ground his wife walked on. Gerry was a solid six feet two, and his tiny wife's constant threats to bash or batter him were a source of great amusement among the staff.

'I bet he was terrified,' she teased Sheree, which was easier than answering the question.

Because she *had* enjoyed the ball. Had enjoyed dancing with Nick, being held by Nick, feeling secure in Nick's arms. Even when he'd been so very angry with her, she'd still felt safe.

Even cherished.

Which was totally off the planet, but a girl could dream.

Nick and Sheree were discussing the food, something Phoebe could barely recollect. She followed in their wake, wondering idly what illnesses—apart from love—might include loss of appetite in their symptoms.

The broad-shouldered shape of Nick's back drew her attention and all the fizzy tremors re-ignited along her nerves. Physical attraction, she assured herself.

'We'll both get past this,' he'd said, but she was beginning to doubt she would. Which meant it was going to be a very long six months.

'So what's new with you and Nick?' Jess demanded, when Phoebe once again met up with her in the canteen.

'Do you lie in wait for me?' Phoebe demanded. 'I've worked in the skin cancer unit for the last six months and rarely eaten lunch with the same person twice.'

Apart from Charles, she remembered grimly.

'Nowadays, I seem to meet you here every day.'

'That's because you hadn't made any special friends,' Jess said with the boundless good cheer she radiated so effortlessly. 'Now you've got me, it's natural we should eat together.'

Is it? Phoebe wondered. When you're so obviously happy you make this love thing seem like a good idea?

But she smiled at Jess. 'I guess so,' she admitted.

In the end, she had to admit it turned out well. Listening to Jess talk, whether of work, or Charles—even sex—made the time pass swiftly, and lightened the general gloom of the day for Phoebe.

Lunch over, she visited the ward, to find Jackie absent and Peter sleeping. With nothing else to do, she returned to the clinic and studied the files of patients who were due in that afternoon.

'You OK?' Sheree asked, unknowingly repeating Nick's question of the morning.

'Of course. Why shouldn't I be?' Phoebe replied.

Sheree shrugged.

'No reason, but you seem to have reverted to the Phoebe who first joined us here when you were new and shy. You've lost that sparkle you've had since you got to know us all.'

'Sparkle doesn't do much for the patients,' Phoebe told her, but the words didn't remove the speculative gleam in Sheree's eyes, and Phoebe guessed it wasn't the last she'd hear of the conversation.

Unless she pulled herself together yet again, and dredged up a bit of pretend sparkle. She'd start with a visit to her father. Tonight! Just to remind herself why she shouldn't, ever, be thinking in terms of love with a man like Nick. Then relief that they'd not become too involved would wipe out the regrets and recriminations, and the old Phoebe would return.

But the visit didn't work. Her father was, if only temporarily, very much in love with Mindy, and Mindy was obviously besotted by him, while Beatrice, the prodigy, was adored by both parents. Part of Phoebe hoped this was finally the real thing for her father, but the cynic in her head mocked her sentimentality.

The rosy glow of love doesn't last, it reminded her.

'But the pain sure does,' she told it, as she drove home to the cottage which had once been her haven, but was now a lonely shell.

Misery stalked her all week, though, mindful of Sheree's observation, at work she pretended to a gaiety she was far from feeling. By Friday, the play-acting had exhausted her and, too tired to drive home, she opted for patient visiting instead. She'd go and talk to Peter. Since the night she and Nick had visited him instead of going to dinner, she'd made a point of popping in to see him most days.

Knowing he'd talk about Nick?

Well, probably, she admitted to herself. But surely that was OK? It wasn't as if she was trying to bump into Nick accidentally. He always visited much later in the evening.

'Come in, lovely lady. Tell me what's been happening,' Peter said, as she cautiously pushed open the door and peered around it to see if he was alone.

'Nothing much. We've been busy, but everyone on the staff has been pleased to hear the daily reports on your progress. It certainly looks as if your immune system has finally decided to get its act together.'

Peter smiled at her.

'A temporary reprieve, methinks, but certainly one worth having. How's Jackie?'

Phoebe gave her own report, mostly hear-say, of Jackie's progress. The aggressive che-motherapy Jackie was undertaking had left her without any immunity at all, and she was tem-porarily in the isolation unit.

They chatted for a while, Phoebe telling him the news of other patients he'd met during ear-lier stays in the hospital, Peter making her laugh with accounts of some of his hospital antics.

Then he switched the conversation with a suddenness that left Phoebe floundering.

'Is it Nick making you so unhappy?' he asked, and Phoebe could only gape at him.

Then anger came to her rescue. Why was everyone commenting on her emotions? What business were they of anyone's but hers?

'What makes you think I'm unhappy?' she demanded.

'You've lost your usual sparkle,' Peter pointed out, and Phoebe felt the top of her head about to explode again.

'What am I? Some kind of fire-cracker? A little ray of sunshine who has to glow and glit-ter, day in and day out? I don't know how you all got this sparkling idea. I'm just me, and I'm reserved, and I always have been.'

Peter nodded gravely.

'But your eyes danced, and your lips curled upward, almost as if they couldn't help but smile most of the time.' He paused then added, 'I said something stupid to Nick a while back. Prompted, I realise now, by my own personal upheaval.' He made no move to explain this cryptic comment, merely adding, 'I wouldn't like to think it had rebounded onto you.'

'Whatever you've said to Nick had nothing to do with me,' Phoebe told him, although she remembered the totally weird proposal and Nick's muttered comment about something Peter had said. 'Nothing Nick says or does has anything to do with me.'

She stood up so Peter would understand the conversation was finished. 'And I don't know why you or anyone would think it does.'

On that note, she crossed to the door, tilted up her lips and smiled at him, wondering how one went about putting sparkle in one's eyes.

'I'll visit you again tomorrow if you promise not to bring up this subject,' she said, and Peter chuckled.

'As if I'd dare,' he said, then waved good-bye.

She was through the door and was smiling at the nurse on duty at the desk when Peter's voice called her back.

'If you're coming tomorrow, could you make it about two o'clock?' he said. 'That's if it's not inconvenient.'

Suspicion flared in Phoebe's breast. She walked back into his room.

'You're not setting me up. Arranging for your old mate to be here at the same time, or anything stupid like that?'

Peter shook his head.

'As if I would,' he said, plaintive innocence echoing in the words.

'I wouldn't have put it past you,' Phoebe told him. 'But if you promise you're not, and that time suits you, two o'clock it is.'

'It's not as if I have a life!' she muttered to herself, as she once again walked out the door.

But the 'appointment' aspect of the visit intrigued her, so she wasn't surprised to find an elegant middle-aged woman ensconced in the most comfortable of Peter's visitors' chairs next day. Assuming it was his mother, she acknowledged his introduction to Marion, deposited the grapes she'd brought along on Peter's tray and settled into the second chair.

She was about to utter a harmless remark about the weather when the older woman spoke.

'What a truly beautiful bride you'll make,' Marion said, and while Phoebe gasped and stared and generally stuttered out her astonishment, Peter laughed.

'Don't mind, Marion,' he told Phoebe. 'She does it all the time. Can't see a young woman without rigging her out in bridal regalia. When Nick and I were young we spent years pretending we weren't interested in girls and keeping them out of the house so Marion didn't fill their heads with images of orange blossom.'

'There's nothing wrong with young girls having images of orange blossom in their heads,' Marion said serenely, while Phoebe struggled with the 'Nick and I were young' scenario and wondered where Marion fitted into it. 'Young people might think they don't need romance in their lives, but the world's a poorer place without it.'

She frowned sternly at Peter.

'I know you and Nick laugh at what you call my foolish fancies, but every wedding dress I make is sewn with love, every stitch set in the certain knowledge that the marriages of my brides will last for ever.'

She folded her arms across her chest and nodded complacently. 'So far it's worked.'

Phoebe smiled at her, relieved to find the woman made wedding dresses, which explained her original statement.

'Do you design the dresses as well as make them?' she asked.

'Right from the first sketch,' Marion replied. 'I don't know how it happens but I only need to see a young woman and I get an image in my head of how she'll look at her wedding.'

'You can imagine how scary that was for Nick and me,' Peter said to Phoebe, 'on the rare occasions she caught sight of a young woman in our company. Almost as bad as casting spells.'

Marion chuckled at his horror, while Phoebe again pondered the 'Nick and me' thing. Perhaps Marion was Peter's mother and, because she was obviously a businesswoman in her own right, she preferred him to call her by her Christian name.

'You never looked too scared,' Marion said fondly, then she dug in her capacious handbag and produced a pencil and a small sketch pad.

'While Nick adopted the perfect antidote to my spells by taking out a different woman every night.

'You'll have to excuse me,' she said to Phoebe, 'but when I've got an idea I need to get it down. You've such a serenely lovely face, I'd hate to think I couldn't capture it. You keep talking to Peter. You don't have to sit still or anything.'

Ordered to keep talking, Phoebe found she couldn't utter a word. Fortunately Peter helped out, speaking of Jackie. A softness in his voice alerted Phoebe, and she studied him more closely, seeing the animation with which he spoke of her eventual return to the ward.

'We might both end up out of here at the same time, even if it's a short remission,' Peter said. 'I've been thinking maybe we could take a trip together. Share the time. What do you think Mrs Stubbings would say?'

Now there was hesitancy with the softness and Phoebe felt her heart cramp. Sharing an uncertain future, had the two of them grown close? Was love stronger than the faceless shadow of death? Could it really move mountains?

'I'm sure she'd understand,' Phoebe told him, her voice coming out far too husky for someone trying to be practical. 'Have you got somewhere in mind? Would you like me to do some investigating for you? Come up with some possible destinations?'

Peter's face lit up.

'Would you? I was going to ask Nick, but I know he's likely to disapprove—well, maybe not disapprove but worry. I'd like somewhere quiet—in the mountains. Jackie talks about the mountains all the time. Somewhere we can have all meals provided. We won't be up to too much activity, either of us. And not too far to drive. I'd get a chauffeured car to take us but can't afford to drive across Australia.'

'I know a guest house up at Mount Tamborine,' Phoebe told him. 'It has views to the ocean one way and the distant ranges the other. It's an old Queenslander style house with big verandahs where you can sit, and when you get sick of one view you can walk around the verandah and settle down to look at another. There are a lot of native birds, and little wallabies come close to the house. It's the perfect retreat.'

'Or a honeymoon haven,' Marion said, reminding Phoebe that she and Peter weren't alone. 'There,' she added, and handed Phoebe the sketch. 'You don't have to wear a Marion David design when you get married, but don't you think something like this would suit you?'

A Marion *David* design? This woman was Marion David—as in Nick David—as in Nick's mother, not Peter's?

Phoebe was too confused to even look at the sketch. She passed it into Peter's outstretched hand, muttered something about another appointment, and seeing Peter later, nodded to Marion, then left the room.

Now she thought about it, she remembered hearing Peter was an orphan—parents killed in an accident, hence boarding school—so, of course, it couldn't have been his mother.

It added to the puzzle of the 'appointment'. Why had Peter asked her to visit at a particular time? So she could meet Nick's mother? Or so Nick's mother could meet her?

She tried to recall Nick's words when she'd questioned him about telling his mother about *all* his dates. He'd claimed it was a strategy—obviously one he'd developed to stop her putting ideas of orange blossom and happy-ever-after into the heads of every woman he met.

One which Marion recognised.

So why today's meeting?

Phoebe sighed. The answer was obvious. It was so she could be added to the list—the harem—and thus rendered harmless. Nick and Peter in cahoots as they'd obviously been all their lives.

The realisation was so depressing it all but overwhelmed her and, head bowed under the weight of it, she headed down the corridor towards the exit and the car park.

Nick saw her coming and waited by the door. He could read unhappiness, even desolation, in the way she moved, the way she held her head. Something shifted in his chest and he cursed his own ineptitude. He'd started the damn charade in the first place because he'd hated seeing her unhappy, and had only succeeded in making things worse.

'Phoebe?' he said hesitantly, when it became apparent she was so lost in her own thoughts she was going to walk right past him.

She stopped as if he'd struck her, and her head jerked up, the startled expression in her lovely eyes evidence of how deep she'd been in thought. Then the expression shifted, momentarily, to what looked like pleasure, only to be immediately wiped away by a remoteness so contained he shivered.

'Oh, hello, Nick,' she said, supercool. 'I've just met your mother.'

And with that, she stepped past him, pushed open the door and walked away.

He hesitated, wanting to follow her, to ask if they could talk. Somehow to make things right between them. But the enormity of what she'd told him held his feet glued to the ground. She'd met his mother?

His mother had met Phoebe?

Peter!

He strode towards the ward, murder in his heart. Well, maybe not murder but, sick or not, Peter was going to taste a little of his anger. This plan was foiled when he found neither Peter nor his mother in the room. He paced around the bed, ate a couple of grapes, then idly picked up his mother's sketch pad, which was sitting on Peter's tray.

She'd drawn Phoebe as a bride, but not with a veil. Instead there was a filmy mantle of some kind, softly draped across her head. The dress his mother had sketched was simple, draped as well so Phoebe's lush curves were suggested rather than emphasised.

Nick felt his groin tighten but it was his heart that was more of a problem. It had spluttered into a panicky arrhythmia, causing his breathing to falter and his entire body to grow hot. He dropped the sketch pad back on Peter's table and sat down on the bed, one hand pressed to his chest, forcing himself to breathe slowly, taking in great gulps of air.

Perhaps he'd better see a cardiologist, he told himself, hoping a medical conversation, even with himself, would calm the furore in his body. Carl Simpson would be the man. He'd make an appointment on Monday. Have a thorough check. Do a stress test, the lot.

His breathing was easier now, and his pulse, when he felt his wrist, steady. He was tempted to glance just once more at the sketch, to prove to himself it hadn't been the cause of his panic, but decided he was better getting out of the room before Peter returned from wherever he was.

He'd yell at him later. Some other day.

Like Monday afternoon at five-thirty? Nick, who'd already had a trying day pretending his body wasn't reacting to Phoebe's presence, answered a call to the oncology ward, thinking it was nothing more than routine. But the tension in the air when he entered the ward suggested it might be more than that, and the nurse's signal that he go to Peter's room filled him with foreboding.

But what he found was far from his expectations. Peter was sitting in his wheelchair, and Jackie Stubbings, newly released from Isolation, was in hers beside him—with her mother looming over her. Phoebe was perched on the bed, and Malcolm Graham was standing at the end of it, fidgeting uneasily.

'I suppose you know all about this?' Mrs Stubbings said, swinging around to see who the new arrival was and apparently finding him a satisfactory target.

'All about what?' Nick asked, sneaking a glance at Phoebe who was flushing guiltily.

'About these two going off together, that's what. Jackie's sick. She needs looking after. Even in remission I have to see she eats the right food, I have to tempt her appetite, see she doesn't get tired and make sure she gets enough sleep.'

She shot a look of deep antipathy at Peter.

'I'd expect you to know that, Peter Carter, and be thinking of her welfare, not encouraging her in this wild scheme.'

Nick shook his head, hoping the movement might sort the words into a semblance of sense.

'What wild scheme?' he asked, when the head shaking didn't help.

'Them going off together,' Mrs Stubbings roared at him. 'What other wild scheme do you think I'm talking about?'

She glared suspiciously at Jackie, as if further 'wild schemes' might be written on her forehead.

'Can we start again here?' Nick asked. He turned to Malcolm. 'Maybe you can explain. What's the problem?'

Malcolm shrugged.

'It's really nothing to do with me what patients do with their time when they're discharged. I can advise them about diet and not over-exerting themselves and give them detailed instructions regarding their medication but, as I explained to Mrs Stubbings, I can't tell them what to do or what not to do.'

He hesitated, then added in a mild tone, 'In fact, even when they're in here, I can't tell them that either.'

Which didn't help Nick one iota.

He turned hopefully to Phoebe, who was obviously in the thick of things, although she'd now exchanged the guilty expression he'd thought he'd caught earlier to one of total innocence.

Hugely suspicious!

'Dr Moreton?'

She shrugged the softly rounded shoulders which had haunted his dreams for the past week and looked towards Peter, who nodded and reached out to take Jackie's hand.

Nick was still getting over his surprise at this action when Phoebe spoke.

'Peter and Jackie want to spend some time together when they both get out of here. Not immediately, of course, but when they both get the all-clear. Mrs Stubbings is understandably upset as she's worried Jackie won't look after herself.'

'I'll look after her,' Peter said. 'I'm not a total idiot. I know exactly what she's been through and how important rest and regular meals and taking her medication is.'

Nick was about to voice his opinion when Phoebe spoke again.

'But, not being a total idiot,' she said to Peter, 'you must understand how Mrs Stubbings feels about this, how concerned she is.'

Another pause, but Phoebe obviously hadn't finished what she wanted to say.

'You must realise Mrs Stubbings's priorities have shifted since Jackie was diagnosed. Jackie's welfare has become her life.'

'Like mine became Nick's,' Peter said, and Nick fancied he heard sadness in the words. Then Peter turned to him and said, 'Well, old mate, are you going to add your voice to the dissenter? Are you going to say our going away together for a short time is nothing more than a foolish whim? That people doomed not to live out a normal lifespan shouldn't pretend to normality? Shouldn't do normal things like fall in love?'

Nick felt the air stiffen in the room when the impact of those final words fell on the assembled company.

'Of course you're entitled to fall in love,' Phoebe said stoutly, and Nick was pleased she'd answered. He was too flabbergasted to think, let alone speak.

'And I for one am totally delighted for you,' she continued in her own redoubtable way. 'Where you made your mistake was in not talking this over with Mrs Stubbings earlier, explaining to her how you both felt. Telling her why you wanted to spend time together.'

Nick heard Phoebe's voice grow husky and saw her blink rapidly as if to rid her eyes of tears.

'I think if you had, Mrs Stubbings would be happy for you both. I think she'd agree with me that it's like a miracle to find love flourishing amidst such adversity. Love's not something you choose but something that's given to you. It's like an affirmation of life, and all that's good about it. A precious gift, rare and beautiful, to bless you both.'

She stood up, glared defiantly at Nick and added, 'Well, that's what I think, anyway.' And marched from the room.

Nick opened his mouth but found he had nothing to say so closed it again. His body wanted to follow Phoebe, but his mind suggested there was too much to consider for him to go barging after her right now.

Besides which, Peter needed him.

He turned towards his friend and realised Peter didn't need him after all, except perhaps to remove the other bemused spectators from the room.

For Peter was smiling mistily at Jackie, who was smiling with equal mistiness back at him.

'Well, really,' Mrs Stubbings said, but Nick detected something suspiciously like a sniffle accompanying the words.

'Why don't Malcolm, you and I sit down and talk about some safeguards we can put in place for this pair's grand adventure,' he suggested to the stunned woman. 'I think over coffee in the staffroom. Malcolm?'

Nick took Mrs Stubbings by the arm, cocked his head at his colleague and somehow got the three of them out of the room. But if he'd expected gratitude from Peter, he was doomed to disappointment. Glancing back over his shoulder, it was clear his friend had eyes only for Jackie.

Maybe Phoebe was right and a miracle had happened. Not the miracle he might have wished for, but a first-rate alternative. Something to be going on with while he worked on the other.

But as he made coffee for the three of them, then talked Peter's and Jackie's idea over with Malcolm and Mrs Stubbings, his mind played with other words Phoebe had said. 'Love's not something you choose but something that's given to you. A precious gift, rare and beautiful.'

Had he, somehow, turned down that gift? How did one know? How could one tell?

CHAPTER TWELVE

WHEN Mrs Stubbings had been pacified to the extent that she was planning how to get an assortment of clothes delivered to the hospital so Jackie could choose some new outfits, Nick excused himself and returned to Peter's room.

As he'd guessed, Jackie was gone, but the smile on Peter's face still lingered.

'Mrs Stubbings OK about it?' Peter asked, and Nick nodded.

'We should have done it better, should have given the poor woman some warning about how we felt, but it hit us both so suddenly. Your Phoebe's right, we don't choose love. It's given to us.'

'She's not *my* Phoebe,' Nick protested. 'In fact, as she keeps reminding me, she's immune to men like me.'

'Nonsense!' his old friend said firmly. 'Don't forget I've seen her with you. What about the night of the ball? She was positively glowing.'

'She wanted my body!' Nick muttered. 'Talk about tables being turned! There I was fancying myself maybe slightly in love, and all she wanted was sex.'

'Are we talking about the same Phoebe here?' Peter queried. 'Dark-haired, twenty-something, doctor on your team?'

Nick nodded.

'Then you've got it wrong,' Peter said. 'Maybe she said she just wanted sex, but really meant something else. Women's minds work differently, you know. Though in my opinion you've mistaken what she said—or meant. If she was immune to you, the last thing she'd want is sex. And what's this immunity anyway?'

Nick looked out the window, his mind recalling the debacle the night of the ball. He answered absent-mindedly.

'I've never received a rational explanation for that statement but I guess if your father's on his fifth marriage, it'd make you wary.'

'If that's the case, then being attracted to a man who's seen with a different woman every week would make you even warier,' Peter reminded him. 'But there's got to be something between you.'

'Only when we kiss,' Nick told him, and Peter laughed.

'It's not funny,' Nick said sharply.

'Of course it is. Look at you. You're a mess over a girl with dynamite kisses and you're sitting here talking to me instead of being wherever she is, talking to her. Or kissing her. Get out of here. Now you've sorted out my love life, go find one of your own.'

Phoebe answered the door wearing the old bathrobe Jess had told her needed updating, and immediately regretted it.

Though she could hardly have answered it wearing her red ball gown.

'Aren't you going to ask me in? Or at least say hello?'

She blinked at Nick, and told her heart to be still because it was only natural he'd call. After all, she'd stormed out of the meeting in Peter's room before any conclusions had been reached.

'What happened after I left?' she asked, backing into the hall and waving her hand towards her living room.

Which was as much of an invitation as he was going to get!

She tied the cord of the robe more securely around her waist, mentally shook herself to get rid of the physical effects of his presence in her home and followed him, then felt a moment of satisfaction as he looked around her cosy room and smiled approvingly.

'I didn't really take in much about this room last time I was here,' he said. 'If I hadn't heard the romantic in you in action today, I might have been surprised.'

A huskiness in his voice made her shiver, and to counteract this effect she looked around the room, wondering what was romantic in a room with polished timber floors, a red rug, an open fireplace and two leather recliners by way of furniture.

Perhaps it was the flowers.

'I love flowers,' she said lamely, as any conversational skills she might once have had took flight.

Nick completed his survey of the room and turned towards her.

'I can see that,' he said gravely, nodding towards the bathrobe which was a faded pink with equally faded red roses trailing up from the hemline.

'I—I've just had a shower,' she stuttered, realising how ragged she must look. 'I'll get changed. Or aren't you staying?'

Nick smiled and all her mental warnings followed her conversational abilities out the window. Then he shrugged, and she wondered if he was feeling as unsettled, as uncertain and uncomfortable as she was.

Surely not. Not Nick.

But he said, 'I'm don't know if I'm staying.' Then added, as if to confirm his uncertainty, 'Or if you want me to stay?'

Phoebe looked at him for a long moment. Did she want him to stay?

Whatever his staying might entail?

Her heart, which had settled into a rapid but more regular rhythm, accelerated again.

Forget sex, she told herself. Just think practical. First, you've got the Peter and Jackie thing to sort out and, second, your relationship with Nick, as a colleague, needs some work. This is an opportunity—

'I didn't mean it as a double jeopardy question,' Nick said, hovering near a chair as if he'd like to sit but didn't dare until she gave the word.

'You can stay,' Phoebe said, and Nick chuckled.

'Don't overwhelm me with a welcome,' he said, but he sat, and settled back into the chair as if it had been designed for him.

Phoebe contemplated racing upstairs to get dressed, but getting dressed involved taking off the bathrobe—being naked with Nick in the house.

She shivered again, tightened the belt and remembered her manners.

'Would you like a drink? Coffee? Whisky?'

Nick rejected the whisky, though he'd have killed for one right then. Said yes to coffee then sighed with relief as Phoebe bustled off to the kitchen to make it.

He'd come here to talk—to try to get things back on an even keel between them, perhaps suggest they start again and explore the attraction between them.

But from the moment she'd opened the door in the faded bathrobe, all he could think about was taking it off her, peeling it back to reveal the woman beneath it and making love to her—with her—until both of them were exhausted.

Great approach! he chastised himself, then he tried to remember all the clever things he'd rehearsed as he'd driven from the hospital to Phoebe's house.

'Did World War Three break out in Peter's room after I left?' Phoebe asked, returning to the room and putting not only a mug of coffee down on the side table beside him but a plate of biscuits as well.

Nick sensed a false bravado in the words and wondered if she was feeling as awkward and uneasy as he was.

He tried a smile, but although she reciprocated with a hint of one it wasn't by any means a top Phoebe-effort.

'I think you successfully put a stop to further confrontation,' he told her. 'Especially as Peter and Jackie both seemed to take your words as some kind of blessing and immediately began smiling at each other as if no one else existed.'

He sipped his coffee and eyed Phoebe over the rim, hoping to gauge her reaction.

Couldn't!

'Anyway, as they obviously weren't going to listen to anything from anyone for the foreseeable future, I hustled Malcolm and Mrs

Stubbings out and we all had a natter about how best to organise things for the lovebirds.'

This time he did see the reaction. A real smile that sparkled on her lips and shone so brightly in her eyes there was no mistaking her delight.

'I knew I'd done the right thing, getting the nurse to page you for back-up!' she said. 'I knew you'd put Peter's happiness before any medical consideration. I think Malcolm felt the same but didn't want to argue with Mrs Stubbings.'

Nick felt a glow of warmth at Phoebe's praise—then realised just how undeserved it was. He held up his hand.

'All I did was paper over the cracks. Whatever was resolved came from you.' He took a deep breath, told himself honesty was the best policy, then added, 'In fact, when I realised what was going on—what everyone was so upset about—my first reaction was as bad as Mrs Stubbings's. I thought it was the most ridiculous idea I'd ever heard.'

The words hung between them and a heaviness in his gut suggested he'd just blown any chance he might ever have had of starting over again with Phoebe.

He searched for the words he needed to make things right again, but his thoughts were so muddled he didn't know where to begin.

And if he didn't begin, he'd lose this opportunity. Maybe lose Phoebe, whom he'd never rightfully had but now suspected meant more to him than life itself.

He'd lose the rare and precious gift!

'I met your mother,' Phoebe said, and although he guessed she was only making conversation—filling in the awful void—he seized the cue.

'It's all her fault,' he grumbled. 'This entire mess! Talk about making a botch of things.'

The puzzled expression in Phoebe's eyes made him grin.

'I'm making it worse, aren't I? Just bear with me, I'll get there in the end.'

Uncertainty fluttered like a cloud of butterflies in Phoebe's chest. She sat in the chair opposite Nick, pressed her hands together between her knees and waited.

'If you've met my mother you'll know she designs wedding dresses,' Nick began. 'My father died when I was young, my three sisters even younger. Mum had always loved sewing and it was something she could do at home, so her career choice wasn't all that surprising.'

He hesitated, ran his fingers through his hair and looked pleadingly at Phoebe.

'She was so darned sentimental about them—about her brides and their wedding dresses, and stitching love together. It was as if love was something she was capable of conjuring up and sewing into a dress, for heaven's sake.'

He did the raking thing with his hair again, breathed deeply and plunged on.

'As an adolescent boy it was downright embarrassing to hear her going on about it, but as I grew older I figured it might have been Mum's way of clinging to Dad. You see, he'd died young, apparently before anything disastrous had ruined Mum's rosy vision of marriage as the ultimate commitment to love. That's when the wedding-dress thing began to loom like a huge responsibility. I assume my sisters feel the same way, as they're all still single. But, whatever they feel I knew, whoever I married, Mum would want to make the wedding dress, then it would be up to me to make sure she wasn't disappointed. Up to me to make sure my marriage lasted for ever and ever.'

'That does happen,' Phoebe told him, refusing to consider her own father's disastrous forays into matrimony.

'Yes, but how often?' Nick countered. Then he shook his head. 'Damn! I'm reverting right back to where this all began instead of getting on with the explanation. That's the cynical attitude that started me on my campaign to stop Mum designing wedding dresses for every woman I met. It's what made me use Peter's illness as an excuse to not get too involved with any particular woman. I was assuming I'd fail to live up to Mum's expectations if ever I did.'

He held out his hands, as if passing all his problems to Phoebe.

'Is this going somewhere?' she asked, her heart now tripping with excitement.

Nick looked at her and groaned.

'I have no idea,' he muttered. 'None!'

Once again lean fingers scored tracks through night-dark hair.

'Less than a month ago, I was a normal, well-adjusted male. Or as well adjusted as anyone with a phobia about marriage failure can be. Then I foolishly kissed a colleague and my world turned upside down.'

The husky words skimmed across Phoebe's skin like a cool feather, and hope held her heart to ransom.

'It wasn't until your words today—when you said people didn't choose love, but rather it was granted to them like a precious gift, rare and beautiful—that I figured maybe someone had given me a present, back there in the corridor at work.'

He looked up and met her eyes, held her gaze.

'Is it too late to accept it, Phoebe? Or to at least start again, to explore what seems to lie between us? Perhaps we could begin by seeing how that immunity of yours is holding out.'

Phoebe tried to speak, but no words came. In the end, sensing a terrible tension in Nick—a twin to her own anxiety—she nodded.

Nick grinned at her.

'Was that, yes, it's too late or, yes, we can start again or, yes, you're still immune?' he asked.

She knew she had to answer, but no words would come. So in the end she stood up and crossed the room towards him, knelt down and took his hands in hers, then tilted her head up towards him.

'Let's check out the immunity first,' she suggested, and her lips parted to accept his kiss.

The immunity had obviously worn off, but Nick must have had other doubts he needed resolved. He straightened up, and smoothed his hand across her hair.

'What about Charles? It's not that long since you were fretting over him.'

Phoebe sighed.

'I know. Pathetic, wasn't it?' She looked up, met Nick's eyes, and read wariness behind the lingering excitement. Knowing she had to get this right, she took a deep breath. 'I think maybe, when I met Charles, I was looking for love, Nick. Ready for it. He was so exactly what I thought I wanted...' She ran out of words, wondering how she'd been so blind.

'While I was so exactly what you didn't want?' Nick said gently.

'What I *thought* I didn't want,' Phoebe told him. 'Tall, dark and dangerous—a playboy like my father. That'll teach me not to judge a book by its cover!'

'And now?' Nick prompted.

Phoebe grinned at him.

'I guess now I'll have to read the book.'

Six months of exploration passed quickly and Phoebe, who'd been accepted into a training position in a busy general practice, was saying goodbye to all the patients she'd come to know in her year at the clinic.

'And when are you and Dr David getting married?' Mrs Dixon asked, confirming that gossip was alive and well in this corner of the hospital.

Phoebe smiled then shook her head.

'You know, we've been so busy getting to know each other we haven't had time to talk about it.'

The heat she still couldn't quite control when she considered just how well she and Nick knew each other crept into her cheeks, and she could feel happiness like a drug in her blood.

'Make time,' Mrs Dixon suggested. 'Believe someone who's been around a lot longer than you. Courting's fun but marriage is even better.'

Phoebe pondered this idea later. She was checking that the patient files were all complete before she left, but her mind was on their mutual wariness about marriage.

Nick came in as she was staring blankly at the computer screen. He rested a hand on her shoulder and she covered it with her own, leaning her head back against his familiar body.

'Mrs Dixon says courting is fun but marriage is even better.'

There was silence for a moment then Nick's hand tightened.

'Should we try it?' he asked.

'Risk it, you mean?' Phoebe teased.

He leant down and hoisted her out of the chair, turning her so he could look into her eyes.

'Would it be a risk, sweet Phoebe?' he asked, his voice hoarse with something that went beyond desire.

'Not for me,' she told him.

Nick drew her into his arms and held her close. In his head he saw a vision of Phoebe as a bride—his bride—in a softly draped dress and a filmy mantle over her dark hair. He knew it was a vision of the future.

His future.

'Mum's already designed the dress, you realise,' he murmured. 'Are you game to wear it?'

'I wouldn't wear anything else, Nick David,' his lovely bride-to-be assured him. 'With all that love stitched into it, you'll be stuck with me for life.'

Nick sighed and rested his chin on the glossy brown hair.

'I couldn't think of a nicer fate.'

EPILOGUE

JACKIE CARTER held the tiny baby in her arms.

'Hello, Jack,' she whispered to him. 'I'm your godmother, you know.'

She passed him to Peter, who was grinning with delight.

'Jack Peter David! Talk about plain names. Maybe you can call yourself JP. No, that won't work. Sounds like one of those fellows who's always signing something. Perhaps if they changed it around, made it Peter Jack—PJ— that's better.'

'He'd be called Pyjamas at school,' Phoebe told him. She was sitting up in bed, unable to wipe the smile from her face as she watched these two dear friends lavish attention on her new son. 'Anyway, as Nick says, there's only one Peter in our lives and you're it. Marrying Jackie so we could call him after her was the best thing you ever did.'

She saw the smiles that flashed between the couple, then held out her arms as Peter passed the baby back to her.

'And where is the proud father?' Peter asked.

'Over at the clinic. Where else? Mind you, he did accompany me to hospital, and actually stayed for about an hour, then he remembered something that needed seeing to and disappeared, reappearing only when Jack was safely delivered.'

'Couldn't stand the pace, eh?' Peter said.

'Couldn't stand the pain,' Phoebe corrected, bending the truth because she didn't want to be raising false hope in the hearts of her visitors. 'He's been the same right through this pregnancy. He had far worse morning sickness than I did, and even started labour pains before me. Talk about being in tune with each other!'

'Well, he's made up for his absence with the flowers.' Jackie waved a hand towards the different arrangements which had transformed the room into a floral bower.

'And he's brought champagne to wet the baby's head,' Nick's voice announced, and they all turned towards the door to see him standing there, a heavy green bottle in one hand, and four long-stemmed glasses in the other. 'Plus a little snack for my wife who regained her appetite for food during her pregnancy.'

He winked at Phoebe, no doubt knowing she'd blush at the intimate and unspoken joke. Early in their 'exploration' he'd claimed she hadn't so much lost her appetite as shifted its priorities from food to love-making.

Thinking of it brought back the now familiar surge of love to tighten the sinews in her body. She hoped she wasn't making it obvious by smiling too mistily at him. He crossed towards her, set down the bottle and glasses, then bent over his new son.

'Hey, Jack!' he said, his forefinger stroking the downy cheek. 'I'll only let your mother have a sip or two of the champagne. We don't want to be spiking your drinks at this early stage.'

He lifted the sleeping baby from his mother's arms, and placed him tenderly in the crib. Then he opened the bottle, poured the drinks and raised his glass in a toast.

'To all of us,' he said, and this time Phoebe felt a different skitter of excitement. She sipped her drink and listened to the teasing chatter, happy to be an onlooker until Nick declared she needed rest and ushered her visitors out the door.

'Well?' she demanded when he returned, checked the baby and then settled on the edge of the bed.

He took her hand and she looked into his eyes, trying to read the answer.

Fancied she saw hope.

'It's too early to tell yet, and it will have to be tested, but there's a possibility the new technique of cloning the cells will be more successful,' he said, then he leant forward and kissed her on the lips. 'Thank you for understanding how important it was to me to be in the lab last night,' he murmured. 'I promise, with the next baby, I'll be with you through every second of his or her arrival.'

She blinked away a foolish tear and did the misty smile thing again.

'What you were doing was important to so many people,' she reminded him. She nodded towards the baby.

'Maybe even to Jack, at some time in the future,' she said. 'So how could I not understand?'

Nick took her in his arms, and held her tightly.

'Love's precious gift!' he murmured, and she knew he wasn't talking about her or the baby, but about the happiness they shared.

And would share—for ever.

After all, it had been sewn into the stitches of her wedding gown!

MEDICAL ROMANCE™

Large Print

Titles for the next three months...

May

EMERGENCY WEDDING	Marion Lennox
A NURSE'S PATIENCE	Jessica Matthews
MIDWIFE AND MOTHER	Lilian Darcy
ENGAGING DR DRISCOLL	Barbara Hart

June

THE PERFECT CHRISTMAS	Caroline Anderson
MISTLETOE MOTHER	Josie Metcalfe
THE TEMPTATION TEST	Meredith Webber
THE BABY ISSUE	Jennifer Taylor

July

DOCTOR IN DANGER	Alison Roberts
THE NURSE'S CHALLENGE	Abigail Gordon
MARRIAGE AND MATERNITY	Gill Sanderson
THE MIDWIFE BRIDE	Janet Ferguson

MILLS & BOON®

Makes any time special™